Shipwreck on Lysithea

Mastery of the Stars, Volume 4

M J Dees

Published by M J Dees, 2020.

This is a work of fiction. Similarities to real people, places, or events are entirely coincidental.

SHIPWRECK ON LYSITHEA

First edition. August 30, 2020.

ISBN: 978-1393122593

Written by M J Dees.

Get an exclusive bonus chapter to this book for FREE!

Sign up for the no-spam newsletter and get the bonus chapter for free
Details can be found at the end of **Shipwreck On Lysithea**

CHAPTER 1: THE SECRET ENEMY

Tori sat in the weapons chair, staring out the observation window. He was fiddling with a small piece of metal; it was a lump of shrapnel they had dug out of him after the accident. He placed it on the control panel and sighed.

It had been a long night, and it was time for Ay-ttho to relieve him. He thought Ay-ttho's obsession with security was unnecessary. They had followed the presidential convoy all the way to the planet Future without attempting to hide and the President had granted them permission to land, make repairs and take on supplies, so why the paranoia?

The unusual signals they had detected had spooked Ay-ttho. That could be the only explanation. There was nothing to fear from the President. They had to flee with him when Barnes obliterated Atlas so he was on their side, wasn't he?

"Who's there?" said Ay-ttho, entering the bridge.

"Identify yourself," said Tori, seeing a reddish purple figure approaching.

"Identify yourself."

"Ay-ttho?"

"The same."

"You are very prompt," Tori checked the instruments on the control panel. "It's exactly time for your watch."

"Get some rest, Tori," Ay-ttho slumped into the pilot's chair, her antennae flopping over the side of her face.

"Great, I'm fed up of this stupid watch business," Tori grimaced with all three sets of his teeth.

"Nothing happened then?"

"Nothing."

"Get some rest then. If you see Sevan, tell him to hurry."

"I can hear him now."

Sevan sauntered onto the bridge.

"Morning Ron," said Sevan, still half asleep.

"Good morning Sevan," said Ron, the ship's navigational computer.

"You're not going to say good morning to us then?" asked Tori.

"Good morning Tori and Ay-ttho," said Ron.

"Not you, Ron. Sevan."

Sevan squinted at Tori, not understanding the point.

"Oh, I'm off to bed." Tori stomped off the bridge.

"Sleep well," said Ron cheerily.

Sevan slumped in the weapons chair that Tori had only recently vacated and stared out of the observation window at the towering buildings which seemed to cover every available space on Future, the planet which served as capital for the Republic.

"Don't let Tori see you there," Ay-ttho warned.

"He doesn't frighten me," Sevan retorted.

Tori stomped back onto the bridge, and Sevan leapt out of the chair. Tori marched towards him but stopped short, retrieving a small object from the control panel which he pocketed before turning about face and stomping off again.

Sevan breathed a sigh before going to sit in another chair.

"What's up with him?" asked Sevan, gesturing in the direction Tori had just left.

"I think he's upset because I made him take the night watch."

"I don't blame him. I'm not entirely sure why you are so worried, Ay-ttho."

"I told you, I don't trust President Man," Ay-ttho looked like she was fed-up of explaining herself. "I don't want to spend any longer on this planet than we absolutely have to. Once we have finished the repairs and restocked, we can leave."

Sevan liked the sound of this. He was very keen to get back to his home, The Doomed Planet, and visit his aunt. Now that Barnes had destroyed the jump point via Atlas, it meant they must travel the long way round and Sevan was keen to get started as soon as possible. In fact, Barnes, head of the Corporation and Sevan`s creator, had destroyed the entire planet of Atlas, or at least moved it somewhere else.

"Then there's the unusual signals that Ron has been detecting," Ay-ttho continued. "I won't be happy until I know what they are."

"Couldn't Ron have just woken Tori if the signal appeared again?"

Ay-ttho gave Sevan a look which suggested he was being stupid to assume that they could trust Ron with such an important task.

"So Tori detected nothing," Sevan felt he was stating the obvious and knew how much that annoyed Ay-ttho. He shut up.

"Sevan thinks I am imagining things," said Ron. "I've detected the signal twice and will show it to you when I find it again."

"There is no signal," Sevan taunted.

"Shut up, the pair of you, you're making my marbles ache," complained Ay-ttho, rubbing the ends of her antennae. "I was here the last time Ron detected it, remember? But he lost it."

Ron was silent. Sevan imagined that if it was possible for a navigational computer to feel embarrassed, then this was it.

A light started flashing on one of the control panels and a screen crackled to life.

"I have detected the signal," said Ron with pride.

"It's the same signal," said Ay-ttho. "A holographic message, but there is nothing there, just gas."

"Gas?" Sevan looked carefully at the image. "It looks like the President, he's made of gas."

"It does look like the President," said Ay-ttho, turning her head at an angle.

"You get on with the President, Sevan," said Ron. "See if you can communicate with it."

"It's not exactly like the President," said Ay-ttho.

"Why do I have to communicate with it?" Sevan backed away from the screen.

"It looks like it's trying to communicate," said Ay-ttho.

"Use the terminals, Sevan," said Ron.

Sevan attached the terminals to his antennae.

"Who are you?" Sevan asked.

"You've upset it," said Ron.

"The signal's fading," said Ay-ttho.

The screen crackled and went blank.

"It's gone." Ron was disappointed.

"Are you okay, Sevan?" asked Ay-ttho. "You look a paler shade of turquoise than normal."

"It looked like the President," said Ron.

"As much as you look like a navigation computer," said Sevan, starting to remove the terminals from his antennae.

"That's the third time we've lost the signal," Ron complained.

"I've got an unpleasant feeling about this," said Sevan. "Ozli has been telling me about rumours of other galactic regions hatching plans to reclaim territories they lost to the Republic."

"And how does he know who is hatching plans about who?" Ay-ttho was cynical.

"He is the President's nephew."

The screen crackled to life once more.

"Here it is again," said Sevan, hurriedly replacing the terminals on his antennae. "Speak to me."

"It's not speaking," it was Ron's turn to state the obvious.

The screen went blank.

"It was definitely a ball of gas," said Ay-ttho.

"I'll ask Ozli to come and see if he can communicate with it," said Sevan. "In the name of the Giant Cup, I'm late!"

Sevan began ripping the terminals from his antennae.

"Ozli invited me to a function. The president and Ozli's mother, they'll be there. There will be lots of important dignitaries. I've got to go."

Sevan ran off the bridge, through the corridors and down the gangplank of the Mastery of the Stars into the hangar where he could see two Republic guards approaching the ship.

"Sevan?" one guard asked as he drew closer.

Sevan nodded.

"Follow us, Ozli sent us to take you to the ceremony."

Sevan followed them onto a shuttle. When he had been Chief Council Member on The Doomed Planet, he thought his shuttle had been the most luxurious he had ever seen, but this presidential shuttle completely eclipsed his in terms of elegance and comfort.

"Is there any..." Sevan didn't have to finish his sentence. One of the shuttle staff opened a cupboard and took out a bottle of the substance Sevan hadn't even needed to ask for, his favourite drink, pish.

The staff member gestured for Sevan to sit in a comfortable chair and then handed him an enormous cup filled with the scarlet liquid. Sevan drank three before the shuttle arrived at the presidential palace.

As he disembarked from the shuttle, Sevan saw that Ozli was waiting for him, in his special vehicle which protected his gaseous form from diffusing into the atmosphere.

"Sorry I'm late," said Sevan.

"Don't be silly," Ozli spoke through his vehicle. "You are right on time, let's go."

Sevan followed Ozli's vehicle along a huge hallway which led to an enormous hall. A smell reminded Sevan of the first time he had seen the President. That seemed a very long time ago now.

At the far end of the hall, Sevan could see the President, a larger ball of gas inside a contraption which looked like a bigger version of Ozli's vehicle. Another, smaller, contraption connected to it containing a similar, though smaller ball of gas.

"My mother," Ozli said with pride.

A variety of strange beings dotted around the hall whom Sevan assumed must have been the dignitaries Ozli had told him about. There was a musical sound which resonated around the hall and the gathering fell silent.

"Ozli," the President called out through his contraption. "Come forward and bring your friend."

Ozli moved forward, but only a little, Sevan also stepped forward to stay alongside him.

"We grieve for your begetter, Ozli," the President continued.

"He's speaking about the death of what you would call my father," Ozli quietly explained to Sevan.

"And yet, the time for sorrow cannot go on forever, so what better sign for a renewal of our joy than my union with your co-begetter."

"What does he mean?" Sevan whispered.

"He's, what you call, married my Mother."

"So father is begetter and mother is co-begetter, that's sexist isn't it?"

"This is not the time to discuss this," Ozli hissed.

"But even this joy must be short lived," the President resumed. "Because we have intelligence that those who lost territory to the Republic under the previous regime are now minded to take back these regions. They perhaps think the Republic's recent struggles with the Corporation might have weakened it. Therefore, I have decided to send ambassadors to these regions in the hope that they may prevent such attacks."

Sevan noticed three vehicles like Ozli's to the side of the President.

"Who are they?" Sevan whispered.

"That's Kellen Kader," said Ozli. "The President's adviser. Next to him is his son Fenris Kader, and next to him is Zarah Kader, his daughter."

Sevan sensed a change in the tone of Ozli's voice.

"You like her, don't you?"

"Don't be silly."

"You do, you like her. Let's have a chat."

"Shhh, you're embarrassing me."

"I bet she likes you. She's looking this way."

"How do you know?"

"Yeah! You're right, I don't know where she's looking, she's a ball of gas, but her vehicle seems to point slightly this way."

"Yes, it does, doesn't it?"

"Let's go," said Sevan, leading Ozli towards the front of the hall. "What do I have to do to get a cup of pish around here?"

Ozli's vehicle emitted a signal, and a waiter rushed over with a cup of pish which he handed to Sevan.

"Wow, that's impressive," said Sevan, before taking a large gulp. "In the name of the Giant Cup, that is good pish."

"Sevan! Stop! Wait here," Ozli hissed.

"What? What is it? She likes you, you like her, you only live once, Ozli."

Ozli didn't move.

"Oh, I see. You two have a history. Tell me all about it."

"Not right now, Sevan."

Sevan did not pursue the matter because, just as he was about to probe Ozli further, the President spoke once more.

CHAPTER 2: A STAR OF CHANGE

"Fenris," said the President. "Tell me your news, you have something you wanted to ask me?"

"Yes, Sir. I would like to ask your permission to return to the Zistreotov star system. I left to attend your inauguration and now I have a desire to return to this star."

"What does your begetter say? Are you happy about this Kellen?"

"Much as I wish him to stay," Kellen Kader began. "He has worn me down with his pleading to let him go. Therefore, I would be pleased if you would let him go, sir."

"Very well then. You may go, Fenris," the President turned towards Ozli. "Ozli, my begotten."

"He has the audacity to call me what you would refer to as Son," Ozli whispered to Sevan, the bitterness clear in his tone.

"You seem to be very melancholy even though it is some time since your begetter left us for the better place."

"I am fine, Sir," Ozli lied. "My recent trip to Waterfall and the attack at Trinculo still weighs on my vapour."

"I regret you were caught up in that terrible business at Trinculo," Ozli's mother spoke. "It was most unfortunate. But don't dwell on these sad events. All lives must end, everyone must pass to the better place eventually."

"That is true," said Ozli.

"If it is true," said his mother. "Then leave this mood behind and try to move on, as I have."

"I cannot help my genuine feelings, my co-beggeter."

"It is nice and commendable that you have these feelings for your begetter," said the President. "But you know, your begetter lost a begetter, that begetter lost his. And no doubt he did his duty as a begotton, to mourn. But to keep up this mourning, through some kind of stubbornness, that shows disrespect to the better place itself. You suffer from a lack of drive, Ozli, and yet an impatience based your simplistic understanding. I blame your lack of schooling, you must not offend the better place. I ask you, Ozli, to throw off this mood. You must remember you are next in line for the presidency. I will pass the role on to you as a begetter would his begotton. You expressed a desire to continue travelling with the recent friends you have made, but this is contrary to my desire. I would like you to remain here on Future, our begotton."

"Please, Ozli," said his mother. "Do not travel with them. Stay here with us."

"As you wish, my co-begetter."

"Excellent answer, Ozli," said the President. "Stay here on Future, with us. Ozli's agreement has pleased me. Let us celebrate."

The President, Ozli's mother, Kellen, Fenris, Zarah and the rest of the guests left the great hall, leaving only Ozli and Sevan.

"Sometimes I wish I could just diffuse into the atmosphere," said Ozli. "Why is it frowned upon to end our own lives."

"Things aren't that bad, are they?" said Sevan. "Come on, let's head back to the ship."

"I don't see the point of existence any more, Sevan. My father was so good to my mother and I. And she used to dote on him. Yet, he has barely gone, and she has already married my uncle, a Stid Beast would have mourned longer. He might have been my father's brother, but he is not fit to even smell his odour. Mark my words, Sevan, this will not end well but it is not my place to say anything so I must remain quiet."

They arrived at the shuttle which transported them to the hanger where the Mastery of the Stars was docked. Sevan availed himself of the shuttle's excellent stock of pish.

"Welcome back, Ozli," said Ron as they embarked.

"Thank you."

"Hello," said Ay-ttho, seeing Ozli enter the bridge. "How was the ceremony?"

Ozli was silent. Ay-ttho turned to Sevan for an explanation.

"His mother has married his uncle."

"What? I thought his father died only recently."

"That's right."

"Oh, I see."

"What I wouldn't give to see my father again," said Ozli.

"We received a signal of something that looked very much like President Man, perhaps it was your father?" said Sevan.

"What? When?"

"Just before I left for the ceremony. Ron and Ay-ttho had seen it twice before. An image just like you, or your uncle, or your father. We tried to communicate, but the signal disappeared."

"Where was the signal?" asked Ozli.

"We saw the image on a monitor here on the bridge."

"You tried to communicate with it?"

"Yes, but it did not respond."

"It's strange."

"Yes, and I didn't believe it until I saw it myself."

"Are you still searching for the signal?"

"Yes," said Ron and Ay-ttho in unison.

"But you don't know from which star system the signal originates?"

"Not yet."

"I wish I could have seen this signal."

"I think you would have been better placed to decipher it that us."

"Did the signal stay long?"

"It went almost as soon as it arrived."

"It stayed longer than that," Ron and Ay-ttho protested together.

"Not when I saw it," said Sevan.

"I'll watch it if it returns," said Ozli.

"I'm sure it will," said Sevan.

"I hope it is my father's image."

"It will return," said Ron.

"Then I will stay and keep watch until it does."

The others sensed that Ozli wished to be alone and left the bridge.

"This is not a good sign," they heard Ozli muttering. "Something bad is about to happen."

*

Fenris Kader and his sister Zarah were alone in Fenris's quarters while he made his last preparations to leave.

"We have transferred everything to the ship, I'm ready to go. I need this change in star systems, I can't stay in this one any longer," said Fenris. "Goodbye Zarah. Make sure you message me to let me know how you are."

"I will."

"Regarding Ozli, I know he likes you and you like him, but be careful, Zarah, nothing will come of this."

"How can you be so sure?"

"Perhaps he loves you now and his feeling are honest but he is next in line to the presidency, Zarah, and he may not make choices of his own. They won't allow him to decide his union, they will decide his partner based on what is best for the future of the Republic, not based on what he wants. If he says he loves you, you realise that, even if this is true, it is not within his power to do anything about it."

Fenris made his way towards the exit, then stopped and turned back to Zarah.

"Think about how you will feel if you listen to his advances and really fall in love with his uncontrolled harassment. Be afraid, Zarah, fear his advances and stay away from him, keep your feelings hidden."

"I will listen to your advice, Fenris. I know you only have my best interests at heart. But do not tell me how to follow the proper way and then live your life without listening to your own advice."

"Don't worry," said Fenris, turning back to the exit. I have already stayed too long, our begetter is coming. I will say goodbye to you both."

"Come on, Fenris," Kellen said as he paused in the corridor, waiting for Fenris. "Your ship is ready, the crew are waiting for you. Let me give you some advice before you leave. Zistreotov may be a star of change for you, but do not speak your thoughts, Fenris. Be friendly, but only with those whose worthiness you have already tested. When you find someone you trust, do not squander their hospitality. Listen to them but keep your opinion to yourself, listen to the opinions and criticism of others but hold your judgement. Live as well as you can, Fenris, but do not overdo it. You can often judge an individual by the way they live and in Zistreotov there are many generous and friendly individuals, but I warn you, Fenris, not to get involved in lending or borrowing credits because you'll find that those who were once your friend may not be any longer. Be true to yourself, Fenris, and don't be false to anyone else. Have a safe journey, Fenris."

"Goodbye, begetter."

"Goodbye, Fenris."

"Goodbye Zarah. Remember what I told you."

"I will remember."

"Goodbye," Fenris left.

"What did Fenris say to you?" Kellen asked Zarah.

"It was about Ozli."

"I understand Ozli has been paying you more attention recently. Be careful, Zarah. Tell me what is happening between you."

"He has expressed his feelings towards me."

"Feeling? Hah! You are so naïve, Zarah. Do you believe what he tells you about his feelings?"

"I don't know what to think."

"I'll tell you what to think. Think of yourself as a child and imagine that his advances are not honest, he is just playing with your affection."

"He has been honourable in his advances."

"Honourable, you call it."

"I believe what he says."

"It is a trap, Zarah. I should know. Don't believe a word he utters. His desire may produce the most beautiful words but don't trust any of them. Be less open to him, Zarah, talk about higher things than love. Ozli is young, but his position ties him. What he wants to offer you is not his to offer. He might make you many promises Zarah, but they are not his to give. You will be better off ignoring him. Don't waste your time, Zarah."

"Okay," said Zarah.

*

Sevan entered the bridge and found Ozli still on watch.

"Are you still here?" Sevan asked. "Are you not tired?"

"I'm fine," said Ozli.

"No sign of the signal?"

"Not yet," said Ron.

"It was around this time yesterday that Ron first picked up the signal."

Outside the hangar, fireworks exploded in the sky.

"What is that?"

"They are still celebrating the union of the President with my mother. There is a very large feast going on."

Sevan wished Ozli had invited them all to the feast, rather than have them sitting on the bridge, waiting for a signal that might never appear.

"Is it usual to celebrate this way?"

"Yes it is," said Ozli, as if it was an unfortunate thing. "It is more observed in the breaking of the rules of celebration than in observing the rules of the celebration itself."

"How do you mean?"

"They will consume a lot of pish tonight, Sevan, and it has less to do with the President's union with my mother and a lot more to do with the fact that it's another excuse to get drunk."

Now, Sevan really wished he was taking part in the celebrations.

"To be honest, Sevan," Ozli continued. "It is an embarrassment to the Republic that we encourage these drunken feasts. Other regions of the galaxy look down on our base practices. They call us drunkards and slander our good name. It distracts from the achievements of the Republic and reflects badly on those of us who are above such activities."

Sevan didn't feel it would reflect badly at all. He would be happy for others to know him as one who indulges in sizeable amounts of pish and wished he had smuggled some out of the ceremony or off the shuttle.

An alarm, which began flashing on one of the control panels, interrupted their reflections.

"The signal has returned," said Ron.

CHAPTER 3: THE MECHANICAL BOWMEN

"Look!" said Sevan. "The signal."

"Save me from the better place!" Ozli exclaimed. "It is my father."

Ozli moved closer to the crackling monitor where the image shuddered.

"Is it a ghost that has returned from the better place?" Ozli wondered. "Speak to me, my begetter, answer me. What should we do?"

"I'm getting more of the signal this time," said Ron. "I think I might be able to decrypt some audio."

"What is he saying?" asked Sevan.

"I can't hear anything," said Ozli.

"Listen."

"Ron, can you patch the audio into my vehicle?"

"Yes, connect one of those terminals."

A mechanical hand emerged from Ozli's vehicle and connected the terminal cable.

"How strong is the signal, Ron? Can you clean the audio?"

"I can hear something," said Ozli.

"I'm filtering the audio," said Ron. "It should sound clearer now."

"Shhh, I'm listening," Ozli complained.

"Okay, be quiet, Ron," said Sevan.

"You be quiet too," Ozli uncharacteristically raised his voice. "I can hear my father's voice."

"He sounds desperate to hear his father," Sevan whispered to Ron.

"Grab a terminal, I'll patch you into the audio as well," Ron whispered back.

"Thanks," said Sevan, attaching a terminal to one of his antennae. "What is this all about?"

"We're about to discover," said Ron.

"Speak to me, begetter," said Ozli.

"Listen to me," said the image.

"I'm listening."

"I am about to die."

"What? Are you not already dead?"

"Don't be sad for me, just listen carefully to what I am about to say."

"I am listening."

"You must revenge my death."

"What?"

"Revenge his murder."

"Murder? What happened?"

"He has commissioned the mechanical bowmen, to diffuse my existence into the atmosphere. To assume the presidency himself."

"The President?"

"He has desired to dispose of me so he can take my partner and the presidency for himself. The mechanical bowmen are my doom, commissioned by him so that no-one would suspect my death was anything more than a tragic accident. Do not allow this crime to go unpunished, the Republic must not shelter this criminal. You must not allow him to enjoy my position. You must take revenge, but however you do it, I ask you not to harm my partner. I must go now. Please remember me."

The screen and audio crackled into static.

"For the sake of the better place, I will remember you. I will get revenge. Against the President, against my co-begetter. This is why he sent me to Waterfall and why he attacked Trinculo; he wanted to kill me along with the rest of the dignitaries."

"For the love of the Giant Cup!" said Sevan, not quite believing what he had just heard.

"Ozli?" said Ron.

"Ozli? Are you okay?" asked Sevan.

"So that's that then," Ozli sighed.

"Ozli?" Ron asked again.

"I'm fine," said Ozli.

"Are you sure?"

"Who are the mechanical bowmen?" asked Sevan.

"Very good," said Ozli to himself.

"What is good?" asked Sevan.

"No, you will tell someone."

"Not me."

"Or me," said Ron.

"You can keep a secret?"

"We can," said Ron and Sevan together.

"There is a villain in the Republic."

"We don't need a mysterious signal to tell us this," said Sevan.

"Yes, you are right," Ozli agreed. "I think I better leave you."

"Are you sure you are okay?" asked Sevan.

"I'm sorry, I don't mean to get you caught up in all of this."

"There is no need to apologise, Ozli."

"Yes, there is. You need not concern yourselves with this signal. Promise me one thing."

"What is that?"

"Do not tell anyone what you have just seen and heard."

"We won't," Ron and Sevan said together.

"Swear."

"I swear on the Giant Cup, I will reveal nothing," said Sevan.

"I swear too," said Ron.

"Upon your circuitry?" asked Ozli.

"Upon my circuitry."

The screen crackled to life again.

"Swear," said the image on the screen.

"Ha ha, there you go," said Ozli.

"What can I swear on, other than the Giant Cup?" asked Sevan.

"Never speak of this," said Ozli.

"Swear," said the image on the screen, which then crackled and faded.

"This is weird," said Sevan.

"There are more things in this universe and beyond than we can imagine," said Ozli, "And there may be more strange things to come. You must both promise me that if you see me behaving oddly, you will not reveal what you believe the cause of my odd behaviour to be. Swear."

"Swear," said the audio. The screen remained blank.

"Why is the signal still trying to communicate," wondered Ozli.

"I wondered that myself," said Ron. "I've been analysing the signal and the message was pre-recorded."

"So, my father is not alive."

"I'm afraid not."

"And it was not a ghost."

"No."

"Then how was he able to answer me?"

"It just seemed like he was answering you, but actually it was just a recording."

"But what about the end where he was repeating my request for you to swear?"

"I think that was just coincidental," said Ron.

"Who are the mechanical bowmen?" asked Sevan.

"The mechanical bowmen are a troop of elite mechanised troops, often used in assassinations, they are the Republic's special forces. I am not surprised the President used them to murder my father. Do you understand why I rely on your silence, no matter how you might see me behave?"

"Yes," said Sevan and Ron.

"Good. In that case I will leave you for now, speak of this to no-one."

Ozli left the bridge.

*

Kellen Kader had parked his vehicle by the control panel in his stateroom in the presidential palace.

Beside him parked Kader's assistant, M'Nosi.

"I have transferred you some credits to give to Fenris," said Kellen. "And some messages."

"I will make sure he gets them," said M'Nosi.

"You would do well, M'Nosi, to observe his movements before you visit him."

"I intended to do so."

"Find out for me what the representatives of our rival regions are doing and saying in Zistreotov. Find out who funds them and who they mix with. Make sure your enquiries are ambiguous enough so you do not reveal the true purpose of your questioning. Do not reveal your relation to Fenris, imply some distant knowledge of him, you know his begetter, for example."

"You can rely on me, sir."

"Make sure Fenris is not getting into trouble, other than that you would normally expect for one of his age."

"Gambling?"

"And drinking, fighting, swearing, whoring."

"But sir, that would dishonour him."

"We must avoid a scandal, make sure he is not getting carried away in any of these pursuits."

"But sir?"

"I have spoken."

"Yes, sir."

"If you have to lie then so be it."

"Very good."

"And then...in the name of the better place, what was I going to say? What was I just saying?"

"It's okay to lie."

"Yes, because in spreading a few gentle lies, you may find that leads you to the truth, and that is what we seek, no matter how roundabout the way we must go to find it. You understand?"

"I understand."

"Good. Then have a safe journey."

"Thank you, sir."

"Be like him. Observe his ways."

"I shall."

"And let him go his own way."

"Yes, sir."

"Goodbye."

M'Nosi made to leave and, as he did so, he needed to let Zarah pass as she entered the room.

"Zarah, how are you? What seems to be the matter?" asked Kellen.

"I have just witnessed something terrible," said Zarah.

"What has happened?"

"I have just seen Ozli. He was behaving strangely. His vehicle was moving in the most erratic way. It was almost as if he had lost his sanity."

"Mad for your love?"

"I don't know. Do you think so?"

"What did he say?"

"He was very aggressive, and he inspected me. He even held my vehicle with one of his tools and he gave a sigh, so long and piteous that he seemed shattered. Then, he let me go and turned away and left."

"Come with me, I will go to see the President. If this is the madness of love destroying him, it might lead to desperate deeds," Kellen led Zarah from the room. "Have you said any harsh words to him lately?"

"No, and as you advised, I have not been replying to any of his messages."

"That might have maddened him. I am sorry that I had not paid more attention and observed him better. I thought he was just playing and intended to seduce you. Curse my jealousy, though I'm afraid that is common for my age. Let us seek advice from the President. If we keep this secret, it might make matters even worse."

*

President Man and Ozli's mother were within their contraptions in the great hall of the presidential palace when Tafazolli and de Wijs entered.

"Welcome, dear Tafazolli and de Wijs," said the President. "Apart from the fact that we have longed to see you, that we have a task for you provoked us to send for you immediately. You were such wonderful friends to Ozli when you all studied together. Have you heard the reports of his strange behaviour? He does not seem to be the Ozli that we all know and love. We worry that it can't just be the death of his begetter that has promoted this radical change in mood. What else it could be, I can't imagine? I ask you both, seeing as though you know him so well, having grown up with him, to accept our hospitality and stay here in the palace so you might offer him some companionship and gather as much information as you can to find out whether there is something we are unaware of that is affecting him. If we can find out what is troubling him then we might help him."

"Dear friends of Ozli," Ozli's mother began. "He has spoken of you both often and I am sure that there is no-one else that he is as close to as you. We would appreciate it if you were to show us this courtesy to stay with us for a while. Your help will receive the thanks fitting the gratefulness of a president."

"You could command us, rather than ask us," said Tafazolli.

"We both will do what you ask," said de Wijs. "We are completely at your service."

"Thank you both, Tafazolli and de Wijs," said President Man.

"Thank you," said Ozli's mother. "Please visit my much changed begotton as soon as possible, our staff will lead you to him."

"We will help him in any way we can," said Tafazolli.

"Thank the better place," said Ozli's mother.

Tafazolli and de Wijs were led away by the President's staff. No sooner had they left than Kellen Kader entered.

"The ambassadors you sent to the outer regions have returned, sir," he said.

"You have brought good news," said the President.

"Have I, sir? I assure you, I am doing my duty. And sir, that I may have identified the source of Ozli's madness."

"Tell me, what have you discovered?"

"Speak to your ambassadors first, then I shall share my thoughts."

"Very well, bring them in."

Kellen left the room, and the President turned back to Ozli's mother.

"Kellen tells me he has discovered the source of your begotton's madness."

"I doubt it is anything more than his begetter's death and our over hasty union."

Kellen returned with the ambassadors, Lichaj and Mazuch.

"Welcome, my dear ambassadors," said the President. "Tell me, Lichaj, what news do you have from the outer regions?"

"Greetings and good wishes," Lichaj began. "There are movements in the outer regions to try to suppress the desires of those groups who wish to regain the territories they feel they have lost. The outer regions did not wish to attack the Republic, but were actually making preparations against the inner territories. On further investigation they revealed that there were elements which intended to assault the Republic. These elements were arrested but, on their arrest, they vowed never to attack the Republic and have now been funded to make a mission to the inner territories. They asked us to return here with a request to give them safe passage through the Republic so they might attack the inner territories."

"I am pleased that they claim that they do not wish to attack the Republic. I will study their request in more detail and consider it before giving my response. Thank you for your efforts. Go and rest, this evening we shall have a feast. Welcome home."

CHAPTER 4: THE FORGOTTEN

The President and Kellen Kader waited in the great hall until the ambassadors had left.

"This is a good resolution to the business," said Kellen. "I will be brief, Ozli is mad. This madness comes with a cause. I have a daughter who has shared with me, this message: 'You must have come from the better place, I idolise you, Zarah. Within your wonderful vapours etc etc.'"

"Ozli sent this to Zarah?" asked Ozli's mother.

"Wait ma'am: 'Doubt that the stars are fire, doubt that the planets move, doubt truth to be a lie, but never doubt my love. Oh, dear Zarah, I am not good at poetry, I cannot produce art to express my feelings, but that I love you, believe me, goodbye. Yours forever, my dear Zarah, as long as I live, Ozli'. My daughter shared this with me and she has more that she has shared to me as he sent them."

"How has she reacted to these messages?" asked the President.

"You know that I am your faithful servant," said Kellen. "I could have ignored this insignificant love affair, done nothing about it. But even before she showed me the messages, I explained to her that Ozli is in line to the presidency and that she should have any expectations with regard to him. I advised her to ignore his advances and reject any invitations. She did as I asked and, as a result, Ozli fell into a sadness following which things got gradually worse until he entered the madness where he resides."

"You believe this to be the case?" asked the President.

"It sounds plausible," said Ozli's mother.

"I will endeavour to find the truth," said Kellen. "You know that he roams the palace for hours on end?"

"He does," said Ozli's mother.

"I will allow my daughter to meet him and we will observe and see what happens, whether or not he loves her."

"Let's try it," said the President.

Ozli wandered into the great hall.

"There he is now," said his mother.

"Might I respectfully suggest that you both leave and I will greet him," Kellen suggested. "I will communicate with you using our devices."

The President and Ozli's mother agreed and left the great hall.

"Ozli!" Kellen approached the President's nephew. "How's it going?"

"Thank you," said Ozli.

"Do you recognise me, Ozli?"

"You are a pimp, your daughters are prolific breeders."

"Not me, Ozli."

"Then please be honest," said Ozli.

"Honest?"

"Yes, honest. Only one out of ten thousand are honest."

"That is true, Ozli."

"The stars rot the flesh of dead beasts. Do you have a daughter?"

"I do."

"Don't let her walk in the starlight, it is a blessing to get pregnant, your daughter might get pregnant. See to it."

"He talked about my daughter and yet he claimed not to know me," Kellen whispered so that only the President would hear him. "He called me a pimp. I think he is far gone. When I was young, I suffered extremities of love very near this, I will speak to him more."

Kellen followed Ozli who had wandered off.

"What are you doing, Ozli?"

"Words, words, words, words."

"What is wrong, Ozli?"

"Between who?"

"I mean, what troubles you?"

"Slander."

"He is mad, but he also has reason," Kellen whispered to the President before turning back to Ozli. "Shall we go outside, Ozli?"

"To my death."

"I suspect his answers have meaning," Kellen whispered to the President. "His madness appears to give him contentment. I will leave him and try to arrange his meeting with my daughter."

"I will see you later," Kellen called after Ozli, who had wandered off again.

"You will see nothing, except my life," said Ozli.

"Goodbye."

"Old fool."

On his way out of the great hall, Kellen passed Tafazolli and de Wijs.

"If you are looking for Ozli, he is in there," he told them.

"Thank you," said Tafazolli.

They entered the great hall and approached Ozli.

"Ozli!" they shouted their greeting together.

"My best friends," said Ozli. "de Wijs! How are you? Tafazolli! How are you doing? You must think I had forgotten you."

"We are as good as anyone could expect and we don't feel forgotten," said Tafazolli.

"Things are neither excellent nor terrible but somewhere in between," said de Wijs.

"That's good to hear," said Ozli. "What is the news, my friends?"

"No news," said Tafazolli, "All in the Republic is good, I believe."

"Then the universe is about to end," said Ozli. "It is not true. What have you both done so badly that someone has sent you here to this prison, the presidential palace?"

"Prison?" asked de Wijs.

"The presidential palace is a prison. Future is a prison."

"Then the universe is a prison," said Tafazolli.

"A good one," said Ozli. "In which there are many cells. Future is the worst."

"We don't think so," said Tafazolli.

"Then it isn't to you," said Ozli. "There is nothing good or bad about the universe, it's just thinking about it that makes it so. To me it is a prison."

"Is it your ambition that makes it prison?" asked Tafazolli. "Is the universe too small for your mind?"

"For the love of the better space," said Ozli. "They could trap me in a pish nut and be the president of infinite space if I didn't have these terrible dreams."

"Are the dreams your ambition?" asked de Wijs. "The stuff of the ambitious is the shadow of dreams."

"A dream is a shadow."

"True," said Tafazolli. "And I have such little ambition that my dreams are shadows of shadows."

"Then do our beggars have no ambition and are our leaders impressive figures or ambitious actors?" asked Ozli. "I am pestered by the most irritable things in this place. What are you two doing here, anyway?"

"To visit you," said Tafazolli.

"Thank you. Did no-one send for you? Did you come of your own accord? Tell me."

"What should we say?" asked de Wijs.

"Anything. They sent you. You cannot hide your silence. I know that the President and my co-begetter sent for you."

"Why?" asked Tafazolli.

"That is what I want you to tell me. On our friendship, tell me whether they sent you."

"What do you say?" Tafazolli asked de Wijs.

"They sent us," said de Wijs.

"I'll tell you why," said Ozli. "To prevent your exposure, then your secrecy with the President and my co-begetter can remain intact. I have recently appeared to have lost my sense of humour and changed my habits. In fact, this entire universe holds no interest for me. Also, everything in this universe. I am not interested in anything or anyone. Do you doubt me?"

"Not at all," said Tafazolli.

"I sense that you do."

"Are you sure you have no interest in anyone? We understand that they have invited a group of actors to the palace. We know how much you enjoyed the theatrical arts when you were younger. Have you forgotten?"

"What actors?" asked Ozli.

"They are Future's own troop, The Forgotten Theatre Company."

"The Forgotten players? Are they as good as they used to be?"

"Not as good."

"How come?"

"They try to maintain the same standard, but they have a lot of young actors."

"How young? Are they children? Who finances them? What do they do when the company no longer needs them?"

"There has been some controversy about them, it's true."

"Then, is it not strange that the President should invite them to the palace?"

"Here they come," said de Wijs, who had moved to a window.

"Tafalozzi and de Wijs, you are welcome at the palace. Let's meet the actors. I will show you a proper welcome, but I have deceived the President and my co-begetter."

"How?" asked de Wijs.

"I am mad when the wind blows one way, but when it blows from the other I am sane."

Kellen Kader returned.

"Are you well?" he asked as he approached the three.

"Did you hear that?" asked Ozli. "That great baby? I will make a prophecy he has come to tell me about the theatre company."

"Ozli, I have news for you," said Kellen.

"Kellen, I have news for you," said Ozli. "When Pascia N'Sauri was an actor on Future..."

"The Forgotten Theatre is here, Ozli," said Kellen.

"Blah, blah," said Ozli.

"I beg your pardon?"

"Each actor arrived..."

"These are the best actors in the region."

"O M'Zanti, Flame of Supa, what a Stellar Enterprise you had!"

"He had."

"Why? 'One beautiful begotton, and no more, the which he loved very well.'"

"Zarah?"

"Am I not right, old M'Zanti?"

"If you call me M'Zanti, I have a begotton whom I love very much."

"That makes little sense."

"What makes sense then?"

"Why...as the better place knows, and then you know: 'It came to pass, as most like it was,' so goes the devout song. Look, my entertainment is arriving."

The actors of the Forgotten Theatre entered the great hall.

"You are welcome," Ozli called out to them. "Welcome, all of you. I am glad to see you all, good friends. I recognise some of you, even though you have changed since I last saw you. Give me a sample of your work, a passionate speech, something that I might know."

"Which speech would you like," asked one actor.

"I heard you speak a speech once. It was like the finest pish, though I think the population did not appreciate it as they should have. It was excellent work. One speech in it I particularly liked. It was Odubajo's tale to Dicko, when he speaks of Toral's slaughter. If you can remember it, it begins like this: 'The rugged Tomori, like the M'Mineon beast..' no, that's not right, it was like this: 'The rugged Tomori, he whose dark arms, dark as his purpose did the night sky resemble. The New Thyophans besieged the Living City of M'Mino. The M'Mineons withstood every onslaught, and the New Thyophans could not find a way through. All was stalemate until young Tomori came up to present the M'Mineons with a gift as a sign of goodwill,' you know the speech I mean?"

"I do," said the actor. "So the New Thyophans constructed a mighty M'Mineon beast and presented it to the M'Mineon's as a gift. The M'Mineon's were sceptical at first, but, they took it into the Living City. As soon as they did, the rugged Tomori, who had hidden within the beast with the New Thyophan army, leapt out of the beast and slaughtered every one of the M'Mineon's without mercy."

"This speech is too long," Kellen complained.

"Please carry on," Ozli urged the actor.

"And so, through his trick, Tomori delivered retribution on the evil M'Mineon's who had taken his father from him."

"I can't hear any more, I have to go," said Kellen.

"Fair enough," said Ozli. "Just make sure that you treat the players of the Forgotten Theatre very well while the stay in the palace."

"Don't worry, Ozli, I will."

When Kellen had left, Ozli turned to the actor.

"Can you perform that play tonight for the President?"

"Yes, of course."

"Good, I want you to include a special speech that I will write for you."

"As you wish."

"Thank you. Follow Kellen, he will see you are looked after."

The actors did as Ozli instructed and left in the same direction as Kellen.

"My dear friends," Ozli said to Tafazolli and de Wijs. "I will see you later at the performance. There is something I must do."

CHAPTER 5: CATAPULTED TO TOMORROW

Sevan found Ozli wandering the palace grounds, alone.

"I was enjoying a moment of solitude," Ozli explained.

"How are you managing things?" asked Sevan.

"I've been terrible Sevan, I've been awful."

"How come?"

"You should have seen the actors of the Forgotten Theatre, they were here. I asked one of them to make a speech and he did it with such emotion. How can he find such emotion for someone that means nothing to him, that he has never met?"

Sevan shrugged.

"If he can summon that level of emotion for a character," Ozli continued. "What emotion must he display if he felt strongly about something that mattered to him?"

"I've no idea," Sevan admitted.

"Yet, here I am, cowardly moping around, not able to motivate myself for the revenge my father has asked me to seek. I am scared, Sevan, scared to take revenge on that treacherous villain. The victim was my father, Sevan, and yet, despite his own request for revenge, I behave like the lowest of the low."

"I'm sure together we can come up with a plan."

"I have the semblance of a plan, Sevan. The President has invited the theatre and I will ask them to perform something very close to his murder of my father, and then I will scrutinise him to see whether he flinches."

"Sounds like an excellent plan."

"But what if the image was not my father, but someone trying to take advantage of my grief to get me to do terrible things?"

"Don't worry, Ozli. Stick to your plan. You will tell from the President's reaction if he is guilty."

*

The President, Ozli's mother, Kellen and Zarah Kader, Tafazolli and de Wijs were all gathered in the great hall.

"You haven't been able to determine the reason for this apparent madness?" asked the President.

"He confessed that he felt mad," said Tafazolli. "But he did not speak of the cause."

"He's also not too keen for us to question him," said de Wijs. "He is aloof when we come onto the subject of his condition."

"Did he welcome you?" asked Ozli's mother.

"Yes, very well," said Tafazolli.

"But he was forcing himself," said de Wijs.

"He was unwilling to talk," said Tafazolli. "He answered our questions though."

"Did you urge him to occupy himself with something," asked Ozli's mother.

"He was very pleased to see the theatre company," said Tafazolli. "And he seemed very keen on the idea that they would play this evening."

"This is true," Kellen confirmed to the President and Ozli's mother. "He seemed very keen that you should both witness the play."

"That is wonderful news," said the President. "Please continue to encourage him."

"We will," said Tafazolli.

He and de Wijs left the hall.

"Would you mind leaving us too?" the President asked Ozli's mother. "We have secretly asked for Ozli to come that he might 'accidentally' meet Zarah. Her begetter and myself intend to spy on them. We will hide ourselves behind these curtains and see whether his behaviour results from love."

"I don't mind," said Ozli's mother. "Zarah, I hope that your beauty is the happy cause of Ozli's behaviour and that you can bring him back his sanity."

"I hope so," said Zarah.

Ozli's mother left the hall.

"Zarah, come over here," said Kellen. "We will hide. I hear him coming. Let's go, sir."

Kellen and the President left Zarah alone in the centre of the hall while they hid.

"Should I just end it all?" Ozli muttered as he approached the entrance to the great hall with Sevan.

"You surely don't mean that."

"Why should I put up with the insult I have had to suffer every time I see him with my mother?"

"Or you could fight back?

"I'm so tired, Sevan, the long sleep of death would be such a relief right now."

"Don't be silly, what makes you think anything would be better after death?"

"Our people believe in the better place, a dream world after death."

"How do you know that dream won't be a nightmare?"

"I think that's why more don't kill themselves, Sevan. They worry too much about what might happen in the better place and whether it would be better at all. Thinking too much stops us from acting."

"Then stop thinking and act."

Ozli stopped.

"There is Zarah. Would you excuse me, Sevan? I would like to speak with her alone."

"I'll catch up with you later. I'll see if I can find some pish."

"Ozli, how are you?" said Zarah as he approached.

"Very well, thank you."

"I have a gift of yours I wished to return."

"I haven't given you anything," said Ozli.

"You know you did," said Zarah. "And you delivered it with the sweetest words."

"Are you telling the truth?" Ozli laughed.

"What do you mean?"

"Are you beautiful?"

"What do you mean, Ozli?"

"If you are honest and beautiful, then your honesty should have nothing to do with your beauty."

"Does beauty appeal more than honesty?"

"Beauty has the power to make up for honesty, but honesty struggles to make up for beauty. I loved you once."

"You made me believe you did."

"You should not have believed me because I did not love you."

"You fooled me."

"Why don't you join the maidens of the better place in their sanctuary of devotion? Better than begatting evil offspring. I am moderately honest, it would have been better if my co-beggetter had not begotton me. I am proud, revengeful, ambitious with more wrongs than I care to remember. I have more terrible ideas than time to act them out. Trust no-one, Zarah, join the order of the maidens of the better place. Where is your begetter?"

"In his chambers."

"Then shut the door of his chambers so he can't play the fool anywhere but in his own space. Goodbye."

"Oh, Guardian of the Better Place, please help poor Ozli."

"If you form a union one day, Zarah, I will give you a plague as a gift. Better that you remain pure as the maidens in the order. Go to their sanctuary, Zarah, go! Goodbye. Or would you rather make a union with a fool? Go to the sanctuary, quickly, goodbye!"

"Oh, Guardian of the better place, restore Ozli to his previous self."

"You pretend that your immorality comes from ignorance. Go to that sanctuary."

Ozli turned and left.

"What has happened to him," cried Zarah. "In line for the presidency... I believed his advances and now he has left me ruined. I wish I had not heard what I just heard."

Kellen and the President emerged from their hiding place.

"He didn't seem in love," said the President. "And although his words were a little odd, he didn't seem mad. There is something wrong, something which is bothering him, and in case the result might be some danger, I have a plan to prevent any problems. I will catapult him to the space station Tomorrow to negotiate a peace with Barnes and the Corporation. Perhaps the journey and the sights he will experience on the way will settle him. What do you think?"

"It's a splendid idea," said Kellen. "I still think the origin of his grief came from neglected love. Zarah, you needn't tell us what Ozli said, we heard it all. You should do whatever you see fit, sir, but my advice would be that, after the Forbidden Theatre has performed, let his co-begetter encourage him to express his grief. Let her be honest with him, while I hide to listen in to their conversation. If she cannot understand the issue, then catapult him to Tomorrow, or send him wherever you think best."

"I agree," said the President. "Madness in the one in line for the presidency must not go unwatched."

*

As the actors prepared for their performance, Ozli hung around observing and questioning them.

"Did you have time to learn the scene I wrote for you?" Ozli asked. "Perform it lightly, don't be melodramatic. It needs to be smooth."

"I will do so," said the actor who looked like he wanted Ozli to leave him to get on with his preparations.

"Don't be too soft though, use your discretion. It should look natural, both the words and the action. Just don't overdo it. It is important that it makes the audience grieve, not laugh. You shouldn't look like a robot."

"I'll try not to," said the actor, wondering whether Ozli would teach his own co-begetters, co-begetter to suck Screrkroils' birth sacks.

"Don't let your actors improvise, it's important they play the scene as I wrote it."

While the actor tried to extricate himself from Ozli's attention, Kellen Kader entered with Tafazolli and deWijs.

"Kader! Will the President watch the play?" Ozli asked.

"And your co-begetter," said Kellen. "Will it start soon?"

"Yes," said Ozli. "Tell them to hurry."

Kellen left the hall.

"You too, get the actors to hurry," Ozli asked his friends.

"Of course," said Tafazolli.

"Sevan!" said Ozli, seeing his friend enter the hall.

"How is it going, Ozli?"

"Sevan, you are one of the most well-balanced individuals I have ever met."

"I think you must have the wrong individual," said Sevan.

"Don't worry, I'm not flattering you so you'll do a favour for me. I know you have no wealth except for your friendly spirits and you've never asked me for credits. You are not a slave to your passions like others. Sevan, they will perform a play for the President. I have asked them to perform a scene which mimics the method the President used to kill my father. When you see them perform it, observe the President and see whether his hidden guilt reveals itself. I will observe him too and afterwards we will compare what we have seen."

"If he hides anything during this play," said Sevan. "I will blame my own powers of detection."

"They are ready to perform. I must pretend to be mad. Find yourself a suitable place."

The President entered with Ozli's mother, Kellen Kader, and Zarah. Tafazolli and de Wijs also took their places.

"How are you, Ozli?" asked the President.

"Excellent," Ozli replied. "Kellen, you once tried your hand at acting, did you not?"

"I did. There were those who said I was good at it."

"What did you act?"

"I played Smayn, they killed me at Zrugas. Syai killed me."

"That was terrible of him. Are the actors ready?"

"Yes," said Tafazolli. "They are waiting to be told they can start."

"Watch next to me," said Ozli's mother.

"No, thank you my co-begetter. I much prefer the view from here."

"Did you hear that?" said Kellen.

"Shall I move alongside you?" Ozli asked Zarah.

"No, thank you."

"I won't touch."

"No, thank you."

"Did you think I meant to reproduce?"

"I thought nothing of the sort."

"It's a fair thought."

"What is?"

"Nothing."

"Have you been on the pish?"

"Me?"

"Yes, you."

"For the love of the Guardian of the Better Place, I'm the only joker here. What can you do if not be happy? Look how happy my co-begetter looks and my begetter only just dead."

"Not only just."

"Not just? A little longer then and still not forgotten. There's hope a memory might outlive life by half a solar cycle. Let the play begin!"

CHAPTER 6: THE BLIND SPACESHIP

Two actors entered the performance space which they had constructed within the great hall. One actor was wearing a presidential-like seal and was saying goodbye to someone he apparently loved, a lover, or partner. He said his goodbyes and acted, making preparations in some kind of spaceship. While, at one side of the stage, the presidential figure pretended to fly his craft through space, on the other side of the stage, another scene began.

A strange and foreboding character summoned more actors onto the stage. These actors wore costumes which they had not made well but which they had designed to look like the uniform of the Republic's elite force, the mechanical bowmen. The sinister character pointed the bowmen in the spaceship's direction and then watched as the bowmen entered the spaceship and engaged in a ridiculously melodramatic fight with the presidential figure who, despite his best efforts, lost the fight. The bowmen removed the presidential-like seal and took it across the stage where they offered it to the sinister figure. They left together in melodramatic elation, leaving the still body of the presidential like figure lying on the stage. His lover, or partner, returned and mourned, melodramatically, over the loss of her love.

The sinister character returned with the bowmen and lifted the lover from her lover's body, which the bowmen removed from the stage. The sinister character pretended to console the lover but gave her gifts. She refused at first, but soon he won her over and she fell in love with the sinister character. They left the stage together.

"What was that about?" Ozli's mother asked him.

"It is all about sneaky villainy," said Ozli.

"What does this signify?" she persisted.

"We will find out," said Ozli, as another actor approached the stage.

"Will he explain the meaning of the play?" asked Zarah.

"Yes, or at least show you."

"For us and for our tragedy, stooping to your kindness, we beg you to listen patiently," said the actor.

"What is this?" Ozli muttered.

"It's short, Ozli," said Zarah.

"Like your love."

The actor, whose character had been murdered, returned to the stage with the lover.

"The planet has made its journey around the star thirty times," he said. "Since we made our union."

"So many journeys may the stars and planets make," she said. "But you are not the same as you were, I have worried about you. But I promise that if anything happens to you, I shall never make a union with another."

"Be careful what you promise," he warned. "Promises are so easily broken. I must leave you soon and go on a journey in that blind spaceship. It is a perilous journey and you should not worry, but promise me if something happens to me, you will take another lover."

"A curse be upon me if I had a second lover. If I love again, he would probably turn out to be your murderer. And then, every time we made our love, we would murder you again."

"I'm sure you believe what you say, but I'm sure your mind would change if the moment arrived. Strong intentions never last because time makes us forget. Changing social conditions helps to change our emotions."

"I swear, I will never make a union with anyone else if you were to leave me."

"You swear deeply but the time has come for me to go, the blind spaceship awaits."

"Come back to me soon, I am missing you already."

The lover left the stage while the other pretended to fly the spaceship.

"How do you like the play?" Ozli asked his mother.

"She protests too much, I think," she said.

"She'll keep her word," said Ozli.

"What do they call this play?" asked the President.

"They call it The Blind Spaceship," said Ozli. "The play is a metaphor for a murder committed in Puutol. Odubajo was his name, and N'Diaye was his lover. You shall see, we have a clear conscience. Here comes Mbokani, his nephew, dressed as a mechanical bowman."

"You are as good as a narrator," said Zarah.

"I could narrate your love, if I could see it."

"My thoughts are black, I am ready, I have the tools and the time is right," said the actor pretending to be Mbokani in his badly made mechanical bowman uniform. "This is a marvellous opportunity, the perfect time, we are unobserved. We will extinguish your disgusting life immediately."

The mechanical bowmen attacked and then murdered the presidential figure.

"They have murdered him for his title and his property," Ozli explained. "Odubajo is his name. The play still exists in Puutolese. You shall see how the murderer gets the love of N'Diaye."

"What's wrong with the President?" asked Zarah.

"Frightened by blank ammunition?" Ozli asked the President, who was already beginning to leave.

"Is everything okay?" Ozli's mother asked the President.

"Stop the play," ordered Kellen Kader.

"Turn up the lights, let's go," said the President, leaving the hall.

Ozli's mother, Kellen, and Zarah followed him. Even Tafazoli, de Wijs and the actors fled, leaving Ozli and Sevan alone in the hall.

"I think we have wounded the beast," said Ozli. "The message was right, the President is guilty. Did you see how he reacted?"

"I'm still only learning to perceive the emotions of gaseous beings," said Sevan. "But the fact that he left so quickly suggests he wasn't happy."

"About the suggestion of murder?"

"Exactly."

Tafazolli and de Wijs returned.

"Come, let us celebrate," said Ozli. "If the President doesn't like the comedy, then he doesn't like it. Actors! Play some music!"

"May I have a word, Ozli?" asked de Wijs.

"Of course."

"The President."

"What about him?"

"He seems very disturbed."

"He is mad?"

"With anger."

"Why are you explaining this to me? I'm likely to make him even more angry."

"Please be sensible, Ozli."

"I am sensible."

"You co-begetter is very upset, she asked me to come to you."

"Welcome."

"Ozli, if you explain what is going on, I can return and tell her. If not, I'll return anyway."

"I can't."

"Can't what?" asked Tafazolli.

"Explain what's going on," said Ozli. "I am not well."

"Your co-begetter says your behaviour astonishes her."

"But her astonishment has no consequence?"

"She would like to speak with you in her private rooms."

"Then, I will go."

"Ozli, we were once friends."

"We still are, Tafazolli."

"Then tell me the cause of your illness. You may feel better if you share it with your friends."

"I lack ambition."

"You are next in line to the presidency."

"Hmm. Ah! The music," said Ozli, seeing the actors enter with musical instruments. "Can you play de Wijs?"

"No, sorry."

"Go on."

"I really can't."

"Please."

"I've never played."

"It's easy. Look, here is the ultrasonic organ, you pump the air using this bellow."

"But I cannot create a melody."

"How about the gamma-ray bells, then? Or the gravity cello?"

The entrance of Kellen Kader interrupted Ozli.

"Kellen!" Ozli pretended it pleased him to see Kellen.

"Ozli, your co-begetter would like you to speak with her."

Ozli moved over to a window.

"That cloud looks like a Trix'an."

Kellen moved over to the window beside Ozli.

"You're right, it looks like a Trix'an," Kellen agreed.

"Actually, it looks more like a Grexut."

"It could be a Grexut."

"Or maybe an Ugreod."

"It is very like an Ugreod."

"I will go to my co-begetter soon."

"I will tell her," said Kellen as he left the hall.

Tafazolli and de Wijs followed him.

"I must go to my mother, Sevan. I feel like speaking violently to her, but I will use no violence. I will punish her just with my words."

*

The President was in his private control room with Tafazolli and de Wijs.

"I don't like him," said the President. "It is not a good idea to let this madness continue. You will take him via the catapult system to the Tomorrow space station to negotiate on our behalf to end hostilities with the Corporation, I will send you detailed instructions. My position as President may not last, he is too dangerous to remain so close."

"We will prepare," said de Wijs. "For the sake of everyone who relies on your presidency."

"There are many individuals dependent on the presidency," agreed Tafazolli. "When a president dies, there are many people who suffer."

"Safe journey," said the President.

"We will be as quick as we can," said Tafazolli, leaving with de Wijs.

No sooner had they left than Kellen Kader entered.

"Ozli is going to see his co-beggeter," said Kellen. "I will hide myself in her rooms to hear the conversation. I imagine she'll give him some strong criticism. I will report back."

"Thank you, Kellen."

From Ozli's position at the junction in the corridor, he could see Kellen leave. He waited for a moment until he was sure Kader had gone before moving to the entrance of the President's control room where, unseen, he could hear the President talking to someone.

"My crime is rotten," said the President. "It smells all the way to the Better Place. The murder of my kind. There is no way to make this right, not while I am the president."

Ozli could see no-one else in the room. He assumed that the President must have been communicating with another in a different room, or different planet.

"My office and my union," the President continued. "Can I make things right and still hold these positions? This galaxy is full of evil ways and rich criminals who avoid justice and reap the profits of their crimes by bribing their way, but they cannot do that in the better place. There is no deceit there, all must tell the truth about what they have done. I am trapped."

Ozli could see the President was alone and unaware that he was being observed. This seemed the perfect moment for Ozli to exact his revenge and send the President to the better place. He thought it just that as the President killed his father, he should be the one to kill the President.

'It's only right,' thought Ozli. 'To kill him while he is repenting of his actions.'

A weapon emerged from the end of Ozli's vehicle, and he pointed it at the President. He held it there for a moment, waiting for the best shot.

He waited.

And waited.

Ozli retracted the weapon back into his vehicle.

'I cannot do it while he is making peace with the better place,' thought Ozli. 'He will go straight to the other side and reap the benefits of that other world. I must do it when he himself is doing terrible deeds so that when he arrives in the better place, the guardian will punish him and will not allow him in the great hall of that other world. I must find him in a moment that has no hope of salvation, so that he falls down into the bowels of the worse place.'

Ozli backed carefully away from the entrance and left.

"I talk of the better place," said the President. "But my thoughts remain here on Future. Words without thoughts never go to the better place."

CHAPTER 7: THE SIGHTLESS SPACEMAN

Kellen Kader entered the private rooms of Ozli's mother.

"Ozli will come soon," said Kellen. "Make sure you deal firmly and speak severely with him. Tell him his games have been too much for others to bear but that you have shielded him from criticism. I hear him coming."

"I will talk to him, don't you worry," said Ozli's mother. "Go, he is almost here."

"I will hide myself like the blind spaceman of the legends who hid and discovered the truth."

"Yes, and we all know what happened to him."

Kader hid himself just in time before Ozli entered.

"What is the matter, my co-begetter?" said Ozli, approaching his mother.

"Ozli, you have offended the memory of your begetter."

"You have offended the memory of my begetter."

"You know that is not true."

"You know that it is."

"How?"

"You do not know?"

"Have you forgotten who I am?"

"No, you are the President's partner, you have a union with my begetter's begetter's begotton and I wish you were not my co-begetter."

"Then I will call someone to correct you."

"Stay here, you are going nowhere. You will not go until you see who I really am and what I am capable of."

"Are you going to kill me?"

"What's happening?" shouted Kellen Kader from his hiding place.

Ozli spun his vehicle round and fired in the noise's direction.

"You've shattered my bioshield," screamed Kellen. "I'm diffusing."

"What have you done?" shrieked Ozli's mother.

"I don't know," said Ozli. "Is it the President?"

"Oh, what have you done, Ozli?"

"What have I done? Almost as bad as killing a president and then having a union with his partner."

"As killing a President?"

"That's what I said."

Ozli went to see who he had shot.

"You stupid meddling fool," said Ozli, seeing the broken vehicle of Kellen Kader. "I thought you were the president."

"What makes you think you can speak with me so rudely?" Ozli's mother asked him.

"You act so innocent," said Ozli. "But your union vows are like a gambler's promises. The guardians of the better place must be blushing."

"At what? What am I supposed to have done, Ozli?"

"Remember, my begetter? He commanded with grace. He was your partner. Now look, your partner, dealing with his co-begotton. Can't you see? What is your interest in him? I'm not doubting you have emotions, but can your desire not tell good from bad? He has cheated you. Could you sense nothing? How could you be so stupid? Are you not ashamed?"

"Don't talk anymore, Ozli," his mother asked. "You make me feel stained."

"Because being in a corrupt union is okay?"

"Stop it, Ozli. Your words hurt. Stop it."

"A murderer, a thief who stole the presidency."

"Stop it!"

"Hang on a minute," said Ozli. "I'm getting a message. Sevan?"

"Ozli, I'm on the Mastery of the Stars," said Sevan. "Ron has picked up the signal again. There's a message coming through."

"Show me."

"Do not forget my message," Ozli watched the flickering image say. "The truth may amaze my partner. You must speak with her."

"How are you?" Ozli asked his mother.

"How are you, Ozli?" she replied. "You seem empty, the way you talk without feeling. Like the blind spaceman woken for battle. Please calm yourself, Ozli."

"Don't talk to me of myths and legends like the blind spaceman. I have a message here that I will share with you. See the pale image. Watch and you will understand why I must have my revenge."

"What are you talking about, Ozli?"

"Can you not see the message?"

"No, Ozli. I see nothing."

"Can you not hear anything?"

"Only you talking to me."

"I've shared it with you, the message from my begetter."

The message crackled and vanished.

"You are imagining things, Ozli." said his mother.

"Imagining things? I am as well balanced as you. I am not imagining things. Admit what you have done wrong, don't make matters worse."

"Ozli, you make me very sad."

"Do not go to the President," said Ozli. "Pretend to be pure, even if you are not. Stay away from him. I must dispose of Kellen. Goodbye for now, my co-begetter. We must be cruel to be kind. Unpleasant things are beginning, but the worse lies ahead."

"Oh, Ozli, what am I supposed to do?"

"Do not go to the President. Do not tell him anything. Do not let him know that I am not mad, but only pretending to be mad. Just like the fable of the blind spacemen who spied on his enemies only to meet his own death."

"I wouldn't know what to say, even if I spoke with him."

"I must leave Future, you know that."

"I heard there was a plan to send you to Tomorrow. Have they agreed to it?"

"The President has sent instructions to Tafazolli and de Wijs whom I trust only as far as I can throw them. They carry the orders. I will go along with them and allow them to dig their own graves, they will find themselves out-plotted. I will drag Kellen into the next room. Goodbye, my co-begetter."

Ozli dragged Kellen's vehicle out of its hiding place and into another room.

He had barely cleared the room when the President entered with Tafazolli and de Wijs.

"Are you okay, my partner?" the President asked Ozli's mother. "Where is Ozli?"

"Please, would you give us a moment?" she asked Tafazolli and de Wijs, who left as she requested.

"What have I seen!"

"What? How is Ozli?"

"He is mad. In a frenzied state of mind, he killed."

"What? Who?"

"Kellen, who was hiding."

"It could have been me. His continued freedom is a danger to us all, to you, to us, to everyone. How should we respond to this killing? Kellen's murder could be blamed on us. We need to keep this quiet. Ozli is mad, and yet our love for him was so great we did not know what was the correct thing to do. Where has he gone?"

"To dispose of Kellen and his vehicle."

"Let us go, my partner. It is getting late. I have plans to send Ozli away and this terrible thing he has done we must just accept," the President turned to the door. "de Wijs!"

De Wijs and Tafazolli re-entered the room.

"Get some help," ordered the President. "Ozli has killed Kellen Kader and has dragged him off somewhere. Go find him and humour him. Recover the body, please be quick."

Tafazolli and de Wijs left the room.

"Come on, my partner," said the President to Ozli's mother. "Let us consult our advisers and let them know what we intend to do and what he has done so we might not be accused of this terrible murder. Come on, let us go, I am very upset."

*

Tafazolli and deWijs found Ozli in a corridor of the presidential palace.

"What have you done with Kellen?" asked Tafazolli.

"Sent him to the Better Place," said Ozli.

"Tell us where he is so we can take him to hold the proper ceremonies."

"Don't believe it."

"Believe what?"

"That I can talk to you and not myself. To be questioned by a Kenzek and me next in line for the presidency."

"You think I am a Kenzek?"

"Yes, I do, soaking up the President's goodwill, his rewards, his influence. He keeps such individuals to be disposed of last. When he's taken what he needs from you, he will squeeze you like a Kenzek and use you all up."

"I don't understand you, Ozli."

"Good."

"Ozli, you must tell us where Kellen is and come with us to see the President."

"Kellen is with the President, but the President is not with Kellen, the President is a thing..."

"A thing?"

"Of nothing, bring him to me."

*

The President was alone in his control room.

"I have sent them to find Ozli and return with what remains of Kader," said the President to the communications control panel. "It is too dangerous to leave him on the loose, we need to put tight restraints on him. He is popular among the idiotic masses, for some reason completely unknown to me, and because of that his punishment would be noted but not his offence. Therefore, his exile must appear planned, we solve desperate problems with desperate solutions, or we do not solve them at all."

Tafazolli entered.

"What has happened?" the President asked him, turning off the communications panel.

"He will not tell us what he has done with Kellen Kader," said Tafazolli.

"Where is he?"

"He is being guarded outside. I came to ask what you wanted us to do."

"Bring him here."

Tafazolli left and returned a moment later with de Wijs, Ozli and two mechanical bowmen.

"Ozli, what have you done with Kellen?" asked the President.

"Getting air."

"Getting air? Where?"

"Not so much that he is getting air, more that the air is getting him. He is blowing on the wind. We avoid the wind at all costs, only to let it carry us off to the better place, in the end."

"That is sadly true."

"We use the air all our lives."

"What do you mean?"

"We use it for ventilation to manufacture the elements we consume, and, in the end, it consumes us."

"Where is Kellen?"

"In the better place, send someone there to check. If they don't find him there, go to the worse place yourself. But if you don't find him there, you might smell him in the corridors to the reception."

"Find him there," the President ordered the bowmen.

"The President won't go anywhere till you come back," Ozli told them.

"Ozli," said the President. "We are genuinely concerned about what you have done and think it would be a good idea if we got you away from Future as quickly as possible. Prepare yourself, your ship is ready to catapult to Tomorrow and a team is assembled and ready, waiting for you there."

"To Tomorrow?"

"Yes, Ozli."

"Good."

"So, you knew of our intention to send you to Tomorrow?"

"I had intelligence of that. So, onto Tomorrow. Goodbye my co-begetter," he said in the general direction of where he thought his mother might be.

"Your step-begetter, you mean, don't you?" said the President, thinking Ozli was referring to him."

"My co-begetter," said Ozli. "Let's go to Tomorrow."

Ozli left the room.

"Follow him," said the President to Tafazolli and DeWijs. "Stay close. Make sure he leaves quickly. He should catapult today. I settled everything that is connected with the affair. Hurry."

Tafazolli and de Wijs did as the President asked and left.

The President turned back to his communications panel and recorded another message.

"If our relationship means anything to you, our agreement, do not be indifferent in this matter. Honour our agreement and ensure that you dispose of Ozli. Do it on Tomorrow. He has become like a disease or a nagging pain, and you can offer the cure. I cannot move on until I know that it is done."

*

As Ozli entered the hangar, followed by Tafazolli and de Wijs, he saw a squadron of military ships with unfamiliar markings parked in the landing bay. He could see a senior commander talking to a subordinate on the gangplank of the largest vessel.

"Speak with the President," the commander was saying. "Tell him that, with his permission, Akpom Chuba would like to take his forces through the Republic. You know the terms of the agreement and the meeting. If the President wishes to negotiate, I am happy to meet."

"Yes sir," said the subordinate.

"Go carefully."

The commander disappeared back inside the vessel and the subordinate descended the gangplank on his way to the hangar exit where Ozli had overheard the conversation.

"Where are these ships from?" Ozli asked the subordinate as he drew near.

"They are from the Cheng-Huang Colony, in the outer regions."

"What is their purpose?"

"We are crossing the Republic to the outer regions on the other side, to the Wreckage of the Arint on Inic B'Campa."

"Who commands them?"

"Commander Akpom Chuba, the President knows him."

"Are you planning to invade the Arint?"

"With no exaggeration," said the subordinate. "We are trying to annex an insignificant part of the region that isn't worth anything. There's nothing there."

"Then the Arint won't defend it."

"They will, it already has a garrison of Arint troops there."

"And your people are willing to die over such a trivial matter? Thank you for your time."

"You are welcome," said the subordinate as he left.

CHAPTER 8: BATTLE IN THE CAVES

Ozli entered the Mastery of the Stars, followed by Tafazolli and deWijs. He found Ay-ttho and Sevan waiting on the bridge.

"I can't believe they talked you into this mission," he said.

"They're paying us, we need the credits," said Ay-ttho. "With the amount they are giving us we should have enough for the journey back home to The Doomed Planet."

"Good to see you too, Ozli," said Sevan.

"How's Tori?" asked Ozli.

"He's doing fine," said Ay-ttho. "He's resting."

"Are we leaving soon?" asked Tafazolli.

"I'd like to introduce you to Tafazolli and de Wijs. They have been friends of mine for as long as I can remember. The President has asked them to escort me to Tomorrow. He has given them special orders."

"Come with me," Ay-ttho gestured to the two friends. "I'll show you the rooms you can use as private quarters in case you need somewhere to relax."

Tafazolli and de Wijs reluctantly followed Ay-ttho, leaving Ozli and Sevan alone on the bridge.

"Everything seems to be going wrong, Sevan," Ozli complained. "But it makes me want to take revenge more than ever. They should give a being of my intellect more important things to do, and yet I don't seem to be able to get around to avenging my father's death. Am I afraid? Or maybe I am trying to plan everything in too much detail. My father is dead, and my uncle has dishonoured my mother and I can't do anything while a squadron out there is about to go to their deaths and for what? For a bit of territory in the outer regions."

*

"I will not speak to her," said Ozli's mother.

"But she is very persistent," said an attendant. "Almost mad."

"What does she want?"

"She talks about her father, Kellen Kader, a lot. She has heard rumours of things being covered up. She gets furious at paltry things. Her speech is very confused, and it takes a while to understand what she means. It would be good to speak to her before she spreads the rumours far and wide."

"Let her come in then," she said to the attendant. "Each slight matter seems to lead to a disaster."

The attendant left and a moment later re-entered with Zarah.

"Where is the President's partner," she said as she entered.

"How are you, Zarah?," Ozli's mother asked.

"How should I know you?" Zarah sang. "By your golden vehicle, with its crystal dome."

"What makes you sing this song? What does it mean?"

"Pay attention, he is gone," Zarah continued to sing. "He is gone to the better place."

"No, Zarah."

"Pay attention, see his crystal dome," she sang.

The President entered.

"See this, my partner," said Ozli's mother.

"Decorated with the sweetest petals," Zarah sang. "To take to the Better Place."

"How are you, Zarah?" asked the President.

"May the guardian reward you with the Better Place," said Zarah. "Though we know that Sagbo was turned into a Taza when the Shoni Mori failed to give enough Lame to the V'Vani."

"Enough talk of myths and legends, Zarah. Talk to me of your begetter."

"Let's not talk about my father. When they ask you about him, tell them this."

She sang again.

"When the star rises again, it will be the day of Taru G'Zone. Early, I will be at your chambers to be your partner. Then he opened the entrance. Let in the partner that would be a partner for sure."

"Zarah!" the President tried to interrupt.

"I will make an oath to New Phaeton and Asum, the young they are to blame. She said before you partnered me in a union you promised. He said: `and so I would have done had you not come.'"

"How long has she been like this?" the President asked Ozli's mother.

"I hope everything will be okay," said Zarah. "We should be patient, but I cannot avoid crying to think he will be in the Better Place. My co-begotton must know about it. Thank you for listening to me. Farewell."

Zarah left the hall.

"Go with her," the President ordered the attendant. "Monitor her."

The attendant followed Zarah out of the hall.

"She is grieving deeply if all that results from her father's death," commented the President. "See, my partner when sorrow comes, it does not come on its own but in floods. Ozli killed her father and now he has gone, and she doesn't even know that he is responsible for his own banishment. It agitates the population of the Republic, although they know nothing about running a region. We have done our best to keep the death of Kellen quiet, but her brother is returning to Future and I imagine that he is considering many conspiracies and does not want to be bothered by the gossip that he must surely be hearing. Facts are leaking beyond the Republic. I hope he does not accuse me. We have already had too many deaths."

"Do you hear that?" asked Ozli's mother, moving to the window. She could hear a sound of disturbance from beyond the palace grounds where caves led to the rest of the city planet.

"It is coming from the caves," said the President. "Where are my bowmen? Let them guard the palace!"

A bowman entered the hall.

"What's the matter?" asked the President.

"There has been a battle in the caves," said the Bowman. "They have breached the boundary. Fenris Kader has arrived with a squadron from Zistreotov. He overpowered the bowmen in the caves. He is on his way here to take the presidency by force and apparently if his coup were to succeed, they would consider it popular across the Republic."

"The Republic is so fickle," Ozli's mother lamented. "What was that noise?"

"They have broken into the palace," said the President. "They will be here at any moment."

They could hear the sound of fighting in the corridor. The bowman went to defend the entrance and was immediately killed.

Fenris entered with a platoon of Zistreotovans. They all stopped when they saw the President with his partner.

"Leave us," Fenris said to the Zistreotovans.

The platoon reluctantly left to wait in the corridor.

"Give me my begetter," Fenris said to the President.

"Be calm, Fenris," said Ozli's mother.

"My reason and calm calls me a fool to be so trusting," said Fenris.

"Fenris, why have you arrived here with what looks like a rebellion? Don't worry my partner, truth is on my side," said the President. "Acts of treason often cannot achieve what they set out to. Why are you so angry, Fenris? Speak."

"Where is my begetter?"

"Dead," said the President.

"But the President did not kill him," said Ozli's mother.

"Let Fenris speak."

"How did he die?" asked Fenris. "At this moment I do not care whether I go to the better or the worse place. I don't care what happens, but I will have my revenge."

"What is holding you back?" asked the President.

"Nothing."

"Fenris, I can see that you are committed to avenging the death of your begetter and who would gamble on you winning or losing?"

"Only his enemies."

"You know who they are?"

"I will find out."

"You are a good begotton, Fenris. I am not guilty of your begetter's death and I am grieving for him too."

There was a noise of a disturbance from the corridor.

"What is that?" Fenris asked.

Zarah entered past the Zistreotovan platoon.

"Oh, my co-beggoton, we will be revenged. Something is wrong. Is it just grief?"

"They took him to the Better Place," Zarah sang. "La, la, la, la. He is in the Better Place."

"Are you okay, Zarah?

"You must sing. Sing and see how the wheel of fortune turns."

"Your nonsense almost makes sense."

"Remember, Fenris. Remember and be sad."

"You don't seem well, Zarah."

"I would give you splendid things, but they all went when my begetter died. They say he had a good end," Zarah began singing again. "Sweet Trani is all my joy."

"You are not well, my co-begotton."

"And will not come again. And will not come again. No, no, he is dead. Go to the Better Place. Never to come back. He is gone. He is gone."

"Do you see this?"

"Fenris," said the President. "I share your grief. It is my right. Go and consult your wisest friends. If they find me guilty, I will give you the presidency. But if not, be patient and we will work with you to get the revenge you seek."

"The way he died. The fact there was no formal service to send him to the better place. I must know why this happened."

"And you will, Fenris. Let the guilty be punished. Come with me and I will explain everything."

*

"What do you mean? We are going to be catapulted to Tomorrow?" asked Sevan.

"There is a portal from Future, almost directly to the space station Tomorrow. The portal takes us from here to Lysithea where there is a portal linked directly to wherever the space station Tomorrow is at that moment. They call it the catapult. They set it when my father was President so he and Barnes of the Corporation could meet in person whenever they needed."

"Brace yourself," said Tori. "We are about to pass through the first portal."

"Where are Tafazolli and de Wijs?" asked Ozli.

"Too late," said Ay-ttho. "We are almost in the portal. I hope wherever they are, they are sat down."

Sevan checked his straps and, as he was doing so, the Mastery of the Stars entered the portal and it forced him back into his seat.

The transition was quick and soon the ship had emerged from the other side of the portal.

"There is Lysithea ahead," said Ay-ttho. "The other portal is just on the other side."

"I have detected a ship approaching," said Ron.

"Did it come through the portal?" asked Tori.

"No, it was waiting on this side."

"Can you identify it?"

"It is a Tenuils pirate ship."

"Tenuils pirates?" asked Tori. "What are they doing this far from the outer regions?"

"They seem to be accelerating on a course to match ours," said Ron.

"Speed up, Ron," said Ay-ttho. "We must get to the other portal before them. They won`t dare follow us in there. Full power."

"We are going as fast as possible," said Ron. "They are still gaining on us though."

"They are activating their weapons systems," warned Tori. "Ron, activate ours."

"All we need to do is get Lysithea between us and them and by the time they have us in their sights we should be at the other portal," said Ozli.

"They are gaining too fast," warned Ron. "They will be in weapons range before we reach Lysithea."

"We have no choice but to try to fight," said Tori. "Weapons almost in range."

"Take us as close to Lysithea as you can, Ron," said Ay-ttho. "We might get some cover."

"They are firing," said Ron.

"Deploy anti weapon defences," said Tori. "I'm locking on target, prepare to fire."

The Mastery of the Stars rocked as anti-weapon devices exploded nearby.

"Fire everything we have," said Tori.

"Their weapons systems are superior to ours," said Ron.

The Mastery of the Stars shook again as another explosion impacted the hull.

"We can't keep fighting them off," said Ay-ttho.

Another explosion shook the hull, and the bridge switched to emergency lighting.

"They have breached the hull," said Ron. "Sealing off the bridge. We are losing power."

The Mastery of the Stars lurched to one side.

"We have insufficient power to escape Lysithea's gravitational pull," said Ron. "We are being pulled into the atmosphere."

"With insufficient power we cannot land," said Ay-ttho. "Ron, prepare the escape shuttle."

There was another shudder.

"Another hit?" asked Ay-ttho.

"No," said Ron. "That was the escape shuttle ejecting."

CHAPTER 9: DESPERATE ALLIES

The President was leading Fenris through the corridors of the palace.

"Now, you must be sure of my innocence," said the President. "We should be friends, Fenris, now that you understand that he not only killed your begetter but wanted to kill me too."

"That seems to be the case," said Fenris. "But why did you not take action against him after he committed this crime? Such a serious crime."

"There were two reasons, which you may consider weak, but to me they were powerful reasons. The first was his co-begetter. She is remarkably close to him. It is a blessing in some ways, but a terrible burden in other ways. We are so close that I could not live without her. My other motive was the opinion of the Republic. He is so well liked in the Republic that they would turn his vices into virtues. Anything I might have tried would have backfired."

"I have lost my begetter, my co-begotton is being driven to insanity. My revenge will come."

"Don't lose sleep, Fenris. I am not so devoid of emotion that I think this matter is trivial. I will tell you more later. I loved Kellen, your begetter, I will not let these crimes go unpunished."

*

Ay-ttho struggled to control the Mastery of the Stars as it descended into the atmosphere of Lysithea.

"How could the escape shuttle eject by itself?" she asked.

"It did not eject by itself," said Ron. "My sensors detected life forms on board."

"Who?"

"Tafazolli and de Wijs."

"I'm sorry," said Ozli. "I will make this right."

"You won't get a chance if I can't land this thing," said Ay-ttho.

"They are still following us," said Tori. "Even if you land her, we'll still have a battle to fight."

The Mastery of the Stars rocked as Ay-ttho struggled to keep her steady. Sevan could see the mountainous terrain coming into view much faster than he would have liked. As the atmosphere thickened and Ron could restore some lost power, Ay-ttho gained some more control over the ship and could guide it away from the mountains towards a dry plain.

"Hold on," she shouted as she prepared for an emergency landing. "This might be a little bumpy."

Through the observation window, Sevan could see the barren landscape passing by at terrifying speed.

The Mastery of the Stars clipped the ground, and it threw the ship back into the air at a perilous angle until Ay-ttho could level her out and guide her down once more.

The hull of the ship dug into the barren landscape, throwing red rocks and dust high into the air. For a moment, Sevan worried that the Mastery of the Stars might somersault, but Ay-ttho kept her level and the ship skidded across the plain, lifting an immense cloud of dust into the air before eventually grinding to a halt.

"Damage report?" asked Ay-ttho.

"We are down to a fifth normal power, they breached the hull, weapons are compromised, and the pirate ship has followed us into the atmosphere," said Ron.

"What?" said Tori. "Where are they now?"

"Coming into land," said Ron.

Sevan unstrapped himself and went over to the observation window, through which he could see the heavily armoured pirate ship landing beside the Mastery of the Stars.

"You may be interested to know," said Ron. "The escape shuttle is heading towards the second portal."

"Take these weapons," said Ay-ttho, handing out blasters.

"They will be useless against the pirates," said Ozli. "I will negotiate."

"Negotiate with Tenuils pirates?" laughed Ay-ttho. "You must be mad."

"Maybe I am," said Ozli, heading for the exit.

"You can't go," said Sevan. "They'll murder you and then they'll murder us."

"Let's see, shall we?" said Ozli. "Ron, would you open the door for me?"

The bridge door opened and Ozli drove his vehicle through.

"Ron, shut the door," said Ay-ttho.

The door shut again.

"We can't let him go," Sevan protested. "They will kill him for sure."

"What are we supposed to do?" asked Ay-ttho. "He does what he wants and anyway, maybe he can negotiate with them."

Sevan rushed back over to the observation window. Ay-ttho and Tori joined him to see Ozli emerge from the Mastery of the Stars and cross the red dirt towards the pirate ship. They watched anxiously as the pirate ship lowered its gangway and Ozli entered; the doors shutting immediately behind him.

"All we can do now is wait," said Tori.

"What do they look like?" asked Sevan.

"Who?"

"The pirates."

"The Tenuils? They are hideous. They say that some have died by looking at them," said Tori.

Sevan swallowed hard. He was at a loss what to do. He tried staring at the pirate ship for a while, but that only made him feel more worried. He would have left the bridge, but as they sealed it off from the rest of the ship, he didn't feel like being separated from Ay-ttho and Tori by a safety door. He felt trapped and looked around the bridge for something to distract him but all he could see was control panels telling him how badly they had damaged the Mastery of the Stars, the weapons Ay-ttho had tried to hand out and the barren dust of Lysithea outside the observation windows.

He wondered what was happening to Ozli on board the pirate ship then he caught himself; he didn't really want to know what horrors the Tenuils might try to inflict.

"Can you scan their ship?" he asked Ron.

"Sorry, Sevan," the computer replied. "The hull appears to have a screening mechanism which is blocking my scanners."

"Never mind," said Ay-ttho. "The door is opening again."

"Already?" asked Sevan, rushing over to the observation window and expecting the Tenuils to toss Ozli's broken vehicle to the ground.

"I don't believe it," said Tori.

The three of them watched in disbelief as Ozli, apparently intact, emerged through the doors and down the gangway before crossing the red dust back to the Mastery of the Stars.

"What happened?" asked Sevan, as Ozli drove onto the bridge before the safety door shut firmly behind him again.

"They will tow us back to Future," said Ozli.

"What?" asked Ay-ttho. "Why would they do that?"

"I explained to them who I was, and that the President would pay a handsome reward for my rescue."

"Will he?"

"Probably not, but I will ensure I suitably reward them. They wanted to kidnap me and charge a ransom but I pointed out that they do not want to draw the attention of the entire Republic guard and that, if they helped us to get the Mastery of the Stars back to Future, I would make it worth their while."

"You negotiated with the Tenuils?" asked Tori.

"They are much more reasonable than you might imagine, and they don't feed on gas, so I was confident they wouldn't try to eat me."

"What about us?" asked Sevan.

"I gave them the impression we were all the same species, so stay away from the windows."

Sevan was the first to move to the safety of the centre of the bridge, Ay-ttho and Tori soon joined him.

"Do they not have scanners?" asked Tori.

"Or eyesight," added Ay-ttho.

"Apparently not," said Ozli. "They agreed to extend their gravitational manipulator to tow us back, and I see no reason to doubt them."

"They could plan to tow us to their lair to eat us," said Sevan.

"If they wanted to kill us, they would have already done it," said Ozli. "When we get to the other side of the portal, I will send a message to Future to explain the situation."

"What about Tomorrow?" asked Sevan. "What about Tafazolli and de Wijs?"

"There is more I need to tell you about them," said Ozli. "But I will tell you later."

*

The President and Fenris Kader were in the president's control room on Future when a guard crackled into view on a screen.

"Yes? What is it?" asked the President irritably.

"We have received a message from the Mastery of the Stars," said the guard.

"The Mastery of the Stars? Isn't that the ship taking Ozli to Tomorrow?"

"Yes, sir."

"Okay, put it through."

A crackly image of Ozli replaced the crackly image of the guard.

"I am returning to Future," the image spoke. "I shall see you when I arrive and tell you my story of my unexpected return."

The screen flickered and went blank.

"What does this mean?" asked the President. "Are they all coming back? Or is it a trick and nothing has happened at all?"

"Are you sure it was him?" asked Fenris.

"It was definitely him. Any ideas?"

"No idea, I'm afraid, but let him come, I would like to confront him myself."

"If you wish."

"Good. So, you will not force me to be friendly?"

"I will not. If he has come back and abandoned his mission and does not intend to return, then I have a new plot ready which he will not escape and they will be able to blame no-one for his death. Not even his co-begetter will suspect trickery. It will look like an accident."

"I would like it better if I could be the agent of his death," said Fenris.

"If it falls into place. Many in the Republic have been talking about you, some of these conversations have been in front of Ozli and they have been very favourable to you. Ozli has not shown the slightest degree of envy except on one occasion."

"What was that?"

"There was once a visitor from Helios Station on Zistreotov. He was fast, you should have seen him at the 100 Q[1]bits Sprint, very skilful, almost as if he was one with his vehicle."

"He was from Zistreotov, was he?"

"From Zistreotov."

"Jahraldo."

"The very same."

---

1.   https://en.wikipedia.org/wiki/Qubit

"I know him very well. He is exceptionally good."

"He spoke of you, Fenris. He said you are very skilled at Jetpack Tag and doubted that anyone could beat you. When Ozli heard this, he became very envious and was looking forward to your return so that he could challenge you."

"I fail to understand the relevance."

"Did you love your begetter, Fenris?"

"Why?"

"It's not that I don't think you loved your begetter," explained the President. "But, in my experience, time dulls its flame. Sometimes delay dampens the desire. What would you like to do when Ozli returns?"

"I would like to kill him."

"Revenge is good, Fenris, but do me a favour. When Ozli arrives, confine yourself to your rooms. When he gets here, Ozli will know you have returned. We will praise you in his presence and stir up the envy once more. Then we will have a competition and gamble on the outcome. Ozli, being careless, won't examine the jet packs so that with ease, or a little shuffling, we can ensure Ozli receives a faulty jet pack. Then, with a deliberate shove, you will revenge your begetter."

"Okay, I will do it," said Fenris. "I know exactly how to adjust the jet pack so that the slightest knock in the correct place will trigger a fatal failure. I'll ensure I do it at such an altitude that it will mean certain death."

"Let us plan further and decide the best time for our plot. If we fail, it would have been better not to have tried at all. We need a contingency plan in case our first fails. Let us, in the refreshment break, supply some poisoned pish that will do the job."

Ozli's mother entered the control room.

"How is it going, my partner?" asked the President.

"Dreadful news follows fast after dreadful news," she said. "It's your co-beggoton, Fenris. Zarah is dead."

"Dead?" asked Fenris. "Where?"

"They found her in the grounds, she had decorated her vehicle with flowers from the grounds and had pierced her own observation dome, mixing her own gas of life with the chemicals in the air of Future which, she must have known, would be lethal for her. By the time they found her, it was already too late. Her living vapours had diffused."

"Then she is dead?"

"Yes, dead and gone."

"Goodbye, I must go."

The President and Ozli's mother watched Fenris leave.

"Let's follow him," said the President. "I have just calmed him down, now I think that will stir him up again. Let's go."

CHAPTER 10: HEADLONG FLIGHT

"Is it going to be a traditional ceremony to send her to the Better Place?" asked a guard, protecting the entrance to the ceremonial garden. "I thought they could only go to the worse place if they took their own lives."

"She is," said the second guard. "They are giving her a proper ceremony."

"How can that be?" asked the first. "Unless she killed herself in her own defence?"

"Apparently, that is the case."

"It must have been self-defence, it can't be anything else. She can't have taken her own life willingly."

"How do you work that one out?"

"If they use a device to pierce their life preserving dome and die, they go to the worse place. But if the object or device comes to them, they are not guilty of shortening their own life and they go to the better place."

"Is that the law?"

"It is."

"Well, it sounds reasonable. If she had not been so high in Republic society, she would have gone straight to the worse place."

"You've hit the Scatan on the Kelxons, there. It's a shame that those higher in the Republic have permission to end their lives as they please."

"Enough of this, I have to go. Enjoy your watch."

The second guard left, leaving the first guard protecting the ceremonial garden alone.

"When I was young and so in love, I thought it was very nice," the guard sang. "To enjoy myself, have a wonderful time. There was nothing as nice."

"Look at that guard singing as he guards the ceremonial garden," said Ozli to Sevan as they entered the grounds from the caves. "Does he have no respect for the memory of those he is guarding within?"

"What is the ceremonial garden?" asked Sevan.

"It is the place where we hold ceremonies to send those who have died to the better place. It is a kind of garden of remembrance, I suppose."

"Maybe he has become relaxed in his duty."

"But as I got older," the guard continued to sing. "Age has held me tight. One day it will despatch me, no matter how I fight."

"Those remembered in that garden used to sing like him," said Ozli. "There are so many remembered inside."

"A weapon slung by my side, to guard the honoured dead," the guard continued to sing. "That they may see the better place, that's way above my head."

"I'll speak with that guard," said Ozli, moving over to the entrance of the garden. "Why are you guarding the ceremonial garden?"

"There'll be a ceremony," said the guard, abruptly straightening up.

"A ceremony? For whom?"

"One of those high in the Republic society."

"Who is he?"

"Not he."

"She then."

"Not she neither."

"Well, who then?"

"She was she but she is no more."

"How long have you been a guard?"

"Since the old president overcame the outer regions."

"How long is that?" asked Ozli.

"Do you not know? It was the same day that young Ozli was born," said the guard, oblivious of who he was talking to. "Ozli is mad, they have sent him to Tomorrow."

"Why was he sent to Tomorrow?" Ozli probed.

"Because he was mad. He will recover there and if he doesn't it doesn't matter."

"Why?"

"No one will notice his madness on Tomorrow. They are all mad in the Corporation."

"How did he become mad?"

"Strangely they say."

"What do you mean? Strangely?"

"I don't really know."

"Do you always guard the ceremonial garden?" asked Sevan.

"Oh yes, I know everyone here and look," the guard allowed them to enter the garden a little. "There are marks for everyone who they have sent to the better place from here."

"Whose mark is that over there?" A tool emerged from Ozli's vehicle and pointed to a mark near the entrance to the garden.

"He was definitely mad, he was. Do you know who he was?"

"No idea."

"He was terrible, poured pish over my head once. He was the President's joker, Gedo."

"He was?"

"He was."

"Ah, poor Gedo. I knew him well, Sevan. A very funny joker, he used to entertain me when I was younger. Where are his jokes now? He was the life and soul of a party. There is no-one to cheer up the presidential palace now. Everyone is miserable. We are all recycled in the end, Sevan."

"Look, over there," said Sevan.

Ozli turned to where Sevan was pointing and saw his mother with the President, Fenris, an official and guards carrying a box.

"What's happening? Is this the ceremony the guard was talking about? Come on, let's hide over there and see what's going on,"

"She should have the ceremony," they could hear Fenris complaining to the official who was a celebrant. "Why shouldn't she have a ceremony?"

"The ceremony will be as elaborate as they have authorised me," said the official. "Her death was doubtful and without the order I would not have been able to offer her to the better place."

"Can we do no more to guarantee her entry to the better place," asked Fenris.

"We cannot disrespect the ceremony."

"You are ignorant," Fenris abused the official. "She will be looked after by the guardians of the better place long after you are suffering in the other place."

"Oh, poor Zarah," Ozli's mother cried out.

"Zarah?" Ozli wondered aloud.

"I wish you could have made a union with my Ozli," His mother lamented. "I thought I would have decorated the ceremony of your union, not attend your death ceremony."

"I wish I could go to the better place with her," said Fenris.

Ozli emerged from his hiding place.

"Who are you to grieve so loudly," shouted Ozli. "I am Ozli."

Fenris moved towards Ozli and activated his vehicle's weapons. Ozli, in turn, activated his.

"Go to the worse place!" Fenris shouted at Ozli.

"You have misplaced your wishes Fenris. Put away your weapons because I am as dangerous as you."

"Split them up," ordered the President.

"Ozli," reasoned Sevan.

"I will fight him," warned Ozli.

"Why?" cried his mother.

"I loved Zarah. Forty thousand co-begottons could not amass the same love."

"He is mad, Fenris," said the President.

"Leave him alone," Ozli's mother pleaded.

"Show me what you would do," Ozli challenged Fenris. "Would you grieve, punish yourself? Drown yourself in pish? Eat a Kaek? I will do all these things. Do you come here to complain? To outdo me with grief? Go to the better place with her, and so will I. You can rant all you want; I can rant just as well as you."

"This is madness," said Ozli's mother.

"Do what you will," said Ozli, before turning and leaving, followed by Sevan, completely bemused by the entire scene.

"Be patient," the President advised Fenris. "Remember what we spoke about. We will put the plan into action as soon as possible."

The President turned to Ozli's mother.

"Come, my partner, let us find where your begotton has gone to in his headlong flight."

Ozli's mother followed the President out of the garden.

CHAPTER 11: THE ASSASSIN

"I am tired, Sevan," Ozli complained to Sevan. "That business at Lysithea was too much."

"I know," Sevan sighed.

"I keep thinking of the battle. That could have been the end for us, Sevan."

"It amazed me that you got us out of there," Sevan admitted. "Every time we take a step towards home, we end up taking one or two steps back."

"I am still troubled by the memory of the fight, Sevan, even though it was nowhere near as bad as the sights we saw at Trinculo. I really thought we would not escape and yet, sometimes our intuition serves us well. When our plots fail, there is something looking after us."

"Are you starting to believe? It was you who negotiated with the pirates, Ozli, not some kind of higher power."

"I'm not talking about the pirates, Sevan, I'm talking about Tafazolli and de Wijs. As we left Future, when they were in their quarters, I accessed the orders they had received from the President to hand over to the corporation on Tomorrow. It was an exact command, Sevan, decorated with all kinds of reasons, talking about the good of the Republic and the good of the Corporation and many terrible things that would happen if I lived. They would have killed me, Sevan."

"Are you sure?"

"I will send it to you so you can see it at your leisure. I thought they had trapped me, Sevan, but I engineered a cunning plan. They had made the first move so, just like a game of Screxels, I had to react. I took the original message, and, with Ron's help, we forged a new message almost indistinguishable from the original but with new orders."

"Why didn't you tell me any of this? What were the new orders?"

"It was a promise from the President, that peace would exist between the Republic and the Corporation as long as the Corporation would execute the messengers delivering the message."

"So, you always intended Tafazolli and de Wijs to go alone?"

"Yes, it was I who organised the attack by the pirates."

"What? You know pirates? They could have killed us."

"Yes, the plan almost went horribly wrong. I couldn't let you, Ay-ttho or Tori in on the plan in case you behaved in a way that made Taffazolli or de Wijs suspicious."

"So, you knew they would take the escape shuttle?"

"Yes, I made sure they knew about it and how to use it. I knew they would."

"Weren't you friends?"

"We knew each other many solar cycles ago but I do not feel guilty for their fate, they knew what they were doing, they were opportunists who did not have what it takes to survive the kinds of games they were trying to play. The President has killed my father, taken my mother, and now he tries to kill me, although I think it is not the first time."

"You think he was trying to kill you at Trinculo?"

"I am sure of it. And to use such trickery. Sending us to Tomorrow for the Corporation to kill us. I will kill him, Sevan."

"But Ozli, he will soon get a message from Tomorrow and find out what has happened there."

"He will, but the meantime is mine. Anyone's life is but a moment, Sevan. I am sorry that I lost my composure in front of Fenris. He only seeks revenge like me. I will be more polite to him the next time I see him."

As they were making their way through the palace, Ozli and Sevan met one of the palace employees, Kirkland, coming from the opposite direction.

"Welcome back, Ozli," said Kirkland as he drew near.

"Thank you. Sevan, do you know Kirkland?"

"No, I don't think we've met."

"Then you were fortunate until now," said Ozli. "He is extraordinarily rich and that is why he roams the palace. Give a Ghot'ok enough credits and they would let him roam the palace. Though this Ghot'ok is generous with his credits, it is true."

"Joking aside, Ozli," said Kirkland. "I have some information from the President."

"I will hear this information. What is it, Kirkland?"

"The President is betting against you, Ozli."

"What do you mean?"

"Fenris has returned from Zistreotov."

"This much I already know. I know Fenris very well, and my experience of him has only been good."

"You like him?" asked Kirkland.

"Why are we even talking about him?" asked Ozli.

"I don't understand."

"If you don't understand, how am I supposed to understand?"

"Kirkland, why did you mention Fenris?" Sevan asked.

"Do you not know?" it puzzled Kirkland.

"About what?" Ozli was losing his patience.

"The President has bet that Fenris would beat you by less than three lengths if he challenged you with the jet pack."

"He thinks Fenris would beat me?"

"He knows Fenris would win but he thinks that you would get within three lengths of him."

"Who says that I would race Fenris?"

"Would you agree to race Fenris?" asked Kirkland.

"If the President wishes me to race Fenris," said Ozli. "Then I will race Fenris."

"May I pass this acceptance on to the President?"

"You can do what you like, Kirkland."

"Thank you, Ozli," said Kirkland, hurrying away.

"He seems in a hurry to get away," Sevan observed.

"I guess it worried him that we might meet his request with a different answer."

Sevan and Ozli continued their journey through the palace, and before long they met another member of the presidential staff.

"Ozli," the member of staff greeted them as he approached. "Kirkland reported to us you will race Fenris. Are you willing to race him now or would you like more time?"

"If he is ready, then I am ready," said Ozli.

"I will tell them," said the member of staff. "They will meet you at the launch pad."

"We will meet everyone there."

"There is something else," the staff member sounded nervous.

"Yes?"

"Your co-begetter, the president's partner, requests that you try to be nice to Fenris before the race."

"How could I not grant such a request?"

The staff member returned the way he had come.

"Do you think Fenris will beat you?" Sevan asked.

"I don't think so. I have had a lot of practise with the jetpack and I doubt he's been racing on Zistreotov. At the very worst, I can stay within three lengths of him. But don't you think it strange that they suddenly want to arrange games?"

"I don't know how things work in your culture," said Sevan. "Everything seems strange to me."

"It might be nothing, but it just seems odd to me."

"Tell them you have changed your mind."

"No, don't worry about it. Let fate take its course. Let's go to the launch pad."

Sevan followed Ozli across the palace grounds to a platform which offered a spectacular view of the buildings which stretched on to the horizon. It delighted him that staff were already there with enormous quantities of pish, some in containers, ready to attach to the vehicle of the sort used by Ozli but also cups, one of which Sevan availed himself.

They hadn't been there for long before the President arrived with Ozli's mother, Fenris, Kirkland and a platoon of guards pushing in two jetpacks.

"Ozli, come here and greet Fenris," said the President.

Ozli did as the President asked him.

"Forgive me, Fenris. I have done you wrong," said Ozli. "Everyone here knows a terrible sadness has troubled me and some might say it drove me to the edge of madness. It was not

Ozli who did these things, it was the madness. I have also been wronged, Fenris, by the madness. I didn't mean any wrong, Fenris, I have hurt you accidentally."

"I am satisfied with your apology," said Fenris. "However, I still have to consider my honour until I receive an expert judgement in favour of reconciliation. But I will respect your words."

"Then let us compete for this wager. Come on, bring us the jetpacks."

"Yes, come on, one for me."

"Your skill on a jetpack is renowned, Fenris. I think you will leave me behind."

"You mock me, Ozli."

"Not me."

"Give them the jetpacks, Kirkland," ordered the President. "Ozli? You understand the bet?"

"I do."

"I have seen you, both of you, Ozli," said the President. "But I think you will find Fenris improved."

"I do not like this pack," said Fenris. "Let me see the other."

"They are the same," said Ozli.

"Yes, they are," said Kirkland, giving Ozli the other jetpack.

"Is the pish ready?" asked the President. "If Ozli wins the first or second lap, I will drink to him. Let us begin, pay attention."

"Let us go," said Ozli.

"Yes, let's," said Fenris.

Staff attached the packs to their vehicles, and they made their way onto the platform to begin the race. Kirkland fired a signal, and they began their first circuit around the grounds of the presidential palace. The gathering watched on gigantic screens which tracked their progress but Sevan realised the entire circuit was visible without use of the screens and he followed the two vehicles, like black dots on the horizon, as they circumnavigated the grounds. As they returned to complete their first lap, there was nothing to tell between them and as they passed the finish for the first of three laps, they both thought they had the lead.

"Ozli leads by a fraction," declared Kirkland.

"Give me some pish. Here's to you, Ozli," said the President as they attached the pish container to his vehicle. "When you finish, there is a container of pish with your name on it."

By the end of the second lap, it was still close, but Ozli was in the lead.

"Another lap to Ozli," said the President. "Replace my container of pish I will drink to him again."

"I will drink to him too," said Ozli's mother, attaching a container of pish to her vehicle.

"No, not that container!" exclaimed the President. "That one belongs to Ozli."

Ozli's mother ignored the President and attached the container to her vehicle.

"It is Ozli's container!" the President shouted to Kirkland. "It is too late."

Sevan looked at Kirkland, who appeared to be more concerned with some kind of control panel.

As they rounded the third lap, the vehicles of Ozli and Fenris came close and their jet packs became entangled in each other's vehicles.

"They are caught together," observed the president.

While they were entangled, Kirkland pressed a button on his control panel and a part of Ozli's jet pack exploded. Fenris's jet pack took the full brunt of the explosion, and there was a second blast as something else on it exploded. Smoke emitted from both packs as the vehicles rounded the last corner.

As Sevan followed the two smoking vehicles, Ozli's mother passed across his sight and he realised there was something strange about her, her gas seemed to be discoloured.

"President! Your partner!" Kirkland shouted.

At that moment, the two vehicles struggled back to the platform and crash landed. When they emerged from the smoke, Sevan noticed that the crash had cracked both life preserving domes.

"Are you okay, Ozli," Sevan asked.

"Fenris? It cracked your dome," said Kirkland.

"I have been caught in my own trap," said Fenris.

"What is wrong with my co-begetter?" asked Ozli, seeing his mother.

"She is perturbed at seeing the cracks in your domes," said the President.

"No, it is the pish. I am poisoned."

Sevan watched as Ozli's mother's gas discoloured and then appeared to evaporate into a purple sludge which condensed on the inside of her life preserving dome before dripping down into a pool in the vehicle's bottom.

"She has been murdered," Ozli shouted. "Who is responsible?"

"I am," said Fenris, his gas already escaping from the crack in his life preserving dome. "You are fatally wounded, Ozli, nobody can help you now. You will be lucky to last minutes;

your gas is escaping from your dome too. We will both die, and your co-begetter too. The President is to blame."

Ozli shot, cracking the President's dome.

"Guards!" shouted the president. "Help me! He's compromised my dome."

"You will be more than compromised," said Ozli.

He used his mechanical arm to remove the half full pish container from his mother's vehicle and attach it to the President's.

Sevan saw the gas of the President react in the same way that Ozli's mother had until the President was only a pool of purple liquid on the floor of his vehicle.

"Justice is done," said Fenris. "Killed by his own poison. Forgive me, Ozli. Mine and my begetter's deaths are not your fault, nor yours mine."

The gas of Fenris rushed through the widening gap in the dome until there was nothing left.

"Go to the better place, Fenris," said Ozli. "I will meet you there. I am going, Sevan. Goodbye, my co-begetter. Sevan, I am almost gone. Report the truth about what happened here."

"I will," Sevan could barely speak the words. "A last container of pish?"

"Give it to me, Sevan. They have dishonoured me today. If you ever liked me, tell my story."

There was a crash as someone opened the platform doors.

"What is that noise?" asked Ozli.

"It is Akpom Chuba," said Kirkland. "He has returned from victory in the Wreckage of the Arint on Inic B'Campa, he comes with Corporation ambassadors from the Tomorrow space station."

"I am dying, Sevan," said Ozli. "I am almost gone. I will not live to hear the news from Tomorrow, but I do predict that they will choose Akpom Chuba as the next president. I support him. Tell him all the events which have brought about..."

Sevan watch with horror as Ozli's gas escaped from the crack.

"Goodbye Ozli," Sevan whispered. "See you in the better place."

Sevan turned to see Akpon Chuba enter the platform with two Corporation officers.

"What has happened here?" Chuba asked.

"What does it look like?" asked Sevan.

"It looks like everyone has died," said Chuba. "What feast must be prepared in the better place for so many lost at once?"

"It is a terrible sight," agreed one of the Corporation officers. "Our message from the Corporation comes too late, no-one survives to hear us, that the order to eliminate Tafazolli and de Wijs has been carried out. Who is going to thank us now?"

"Not from the President, had he been here to thank you," said Sevan. "He never gave the order. But since you have arrived at such a timely moment from invading the Wreckage of the Arint on Inic B'Campa or from Tomorrow, place these vehicles on public view, and let me tell the story of how this came about. You will hear of disgraceful and desperate acts, of murder, judgement, slaughter, cunning, revenge and mistakes which brought revenge on the revenger. I will tell you all of this."

"Tell us now," said Chuba. "We will assemble the most important figures in the Republic. I have some historical claims in this republic and, although I wish it were in better circumstances, I would take this opportunity to stake my claim."

"I also have something to say about that," said Sevan. "But let everyone hear my story now, before more misunderstanding leads to more misfortune."

"Have these vehicles carried to the great hall," Chuba ordered. "Ozli would have made a good President. Let us have a ceremony to send him to the better place."

CHAPTER 12: LOST IN STRANGE WORLDS

"It's not your fault," said Ay-ttho.

"There's no way you could have predicted what would happen," said Tori.

The three friends sat on the bridge of the Mastery of the Stars. They hadn't known Ozli for that long, but they already missed his presence.

"I guess there's no reason for us to stay any longer," said Ay-ttho. "Ozli had the ship repaired and replenished with fuel and supplies. We may as well leave."

"I wanted to attend the ceremony that sends him to the better place," said Sevan.

"Of course."

"What happened to the pirates?"

"They left as soon as Ozli had paid them off," said Ay-ttho. "Straight after we arrived."

"We have a visitor," announced Ron.

"Who is it?" asked Ay-ttho.

"It's Kirkland," said Ron. "He says it's important."

"Let him in," said Ay-ttho.

As Kirkland appeared on the bridge, he seemed extremely agitated.

"What is it?" asked Sevan. "What's wrong?"

"You should leave immediately," Kirkland spluttered out his words.

"We would go straight after the ceremony."

"No, I mean you should leave now."

"Why?"

"It's Akpom Chuba, the power has driven him mad."

"Already?"

"He is blaming you all for the murders of the President, his partner and of Ozli, Fenris, Zarah and Kellen Kader."

"What? All of them?"

"Fine by me," said Ay-ttho. "We need to take the long way round to The Doomed Planet since Barnes destroyed the Atlas portal, so it suits me fine, the sooner the better. Let's leave now."

"No, you mustn't use the long way round," warned Kirkland. "That's where Chuba would expect you to go."

"What's the alternative?" asked Tori.

"You must go via the outer regions."

"Via the strange worlds?"

"The Sirius route," said Ay-ttho. "It's true. Chuba wouldn't expect us to be stupid enough to take the strange world route via Sirius."

"And are we?" asked Sevan. "Stupid enough?"

"Apparently," said Tori after taking a moment to examine Ay-ttho's expression.

"I have no navigational chart for the strange worlds," said Ron.

"That's okay," said Ay-ttho. "We'll ask for directions."

"I wish you the best of luck," said Kirkland. "And, if I were you, I'd never return to the Republic, let alone Future."

"Don't worry, we won't be coming back to Future any time soon."

"But The Doomed Planet is in the Republic," said Sevan after Kirkland had left.

"Don't worry Sevan," said Ay-ttho. "The Doomed Planet is on the edge of the Republic. We can enter on the far side where no-one will spot us."

"You mean we have to skirt around the outside of the Republic until we get to The Doomed Planet?"

"That's about it."

"But how long is that going to take?"

"We're about to find out. Ron, prepare for launch."

Sevan watched the city planet of Future retreating into the distance through the observation windows. He was sad to have left his friend behind, having not even been able to attend Ozli's ceremony, but he was very glad to get away from the capitol planet of the republic and yearned for the more remote systems where he remembered life being quieter.

"Head straight for the outer regions, Ron," said Ay-ttho.

"The nearest portal will take us past the Wreckage of the Arint on Inic B'Campa," Ron warned.

"The battle is over," said Ay-ttho. "The Cheng-Huang decimated them."

"I hope you're right," said Sevan.

As they approached the portal, Sevan gazed through the observation windows with apprehension, wondering what might be on the other side.

"Republic vessels have launched from Future," Ron announced.

"They're coming after us," said Ay-ttho. "There's no going back now."

She had barely finished speaking when the Mastery of the Stars entered the portal. Sevan held onto his chair and at first wished that he had taken some pish from the platform on

Future before remembering what had happened to most who had drunk pish there.

Within a few moments, the Mastery of the Stars had emerged through the other side of the portal and Sevan could see nothing but space.

"Where is Inic B'Campa?" asked Ay-ttho.

"How should I know?" said Ron. "I told you, I don't have any navigation charts for the outer regions."

"Great," said Sevan. "So, we've only just come through the portal and we are already lost."

"My sensors are picking up a planet ahead," said Ron.

"It must be Inic B'Campa," said Ay-ttho. "We need a place to hide before the Republic ships come through that portal."

As they approached the planet, the destruction became apparent. The atmosphere was thick with smoke and, as they descended through the clouds, everything that could burn was burning.

"Did Chuba do all this?" asked Sevan.

"It looks like the Cheng-Huang have eradicated the Arint," said Tori. "And all for the sake of territory."

As the Mastery of the Stars neared the surface, Sevan saw that what was burning was the wreckage of the largest ship he had ever seen.

"What's that?" he asked.

"The Arint were a nomadic tribe," explained Tori. "They had to abandon their home planet many eons ago and travelled the galaxy in search of a new home. Some even say they came from another galaxy altogether. When their ship malfunctioned, they crash landed on Inic B'Campa and for millennia made that their home until first the Republic and then other tribes like the Cheng-Huang expanded their territory."

"The Arint were a peaceful race," added Ay-ttho. "But they took up arms to defend themselves against a series of invaders. Until now."

Sevan gazed out of the window at the destruction of what he imagined must have been countless generations of survival against the odds, all crushed in a relative instant by the Cheng-Huang just because they could.

"Ron? Can you sense anything?" asked Ay-ttho. "Maybe the Arint had navigation charts."

"But they have destroyed everything," said Sevan.

"Ron?" Ay-ttho persisted.

There was a moment of silence while they all waited for Ron's answer.

"Almost all of their computing has been destroyed," he said, at last. "I am detecting a faint signal which could represent some functioning equipment. I will navigate the ship there in the hope we can access their system."

The Mastery of the Stars circled the burning wreckage. Sevan marvelled at how enormous the craft must have been when it was whole, but realised that it would have had to have been huge to transport an entire civilisation from another galaxy.

"We are closing in on the source of the signal," said Ron. "I have also detected Republic ships this side of the portal heading this way."

"We need to land close to the wreckage and activate the cloak," said Ay-ttho.

"What's the cloak?" asked Sevan.

"It's a way that Ron can shield our signals so the scanners of the Republic vessels won't detect us."

"Why didn't I know about this? We could have used it when we were being chased by the pirates."

"It doesn't make us invisible, Sevan, it just screens our electronic footprint so they hopefully will think we are just another part of the wreckage."

The Mastery of the Stars slowed considerably as it approached a section of the wreckage which, though smouldering, had stopped burning.

"I am detecting something in this section," said Ron.

"Land us in that space beneath the bulkhead and activate the cloak," said Ay-ttho. "We will have to wait until the Republic vessels pass before we can investigate."

Ron landed the ship as Ay-ttho had instructed and switch the bridge to emergency lighting,

From outside, Sevan could hear distorting metals, punctuated by the occasional crash of part of the bulkhead collapsing. Soon a different sound, a steady roar, overwhelmed the noise.

"What's that?" he asked.

"That's the sound of the Republic fleet entering the atmosphere," said Ron. "They will circle the wreckage trying to pick up our signal, I'm shutting down all power except for life support."

Ron plunged the bridge into complete darkness, only reflections of the nearest flames provided illumination through the observation windows. They created dancing shadows on the control panels.

Sevan listened as the roar of the Republic fleet drew closer until it seemed on top of them. Sevan, Ay-ttho and Tori looked at each other in silence, all hoping that the fleet would soon pass. They passed so slowly that Sevan was convinced they must have spotted the Mastery of the Stars but after what felt like an unbearable pause; they moved on.

Sevan and the others listened as the roar of the fleet died away until Ron turned the emergency power back on.

"Who's the best navigational computer in the galaxy?" he asked.

"What have you done, Ron?" asked Ay-ttho.

"Tell me," Ron persisted. "Tell me who is the best navigational computer in the galaxy?"

"You are Ron, why?"

"As the Republic ships passed, I picked up their scanning signals and merged something of my own in with the return signals."

"What? Ron, you could have given us away!"

"I matched their signal so closely it would be indistinguishable to them from their own signals. I gave me the cover I needed to access their systems, and I found a route from here to Sirius. I have navigational charts from Sirius to The Doomed Planet."

"Ron! You are a genius," said Tori.

"I know," said Ron.

"Let's give them time to give up the chase, or at least search elsewhere," said Ay-ttho. "Then we can get on our way."

"There is another thing," said Ron. "The readings I was picking up before. I don't think the computer systems of the wreck made them."

"What do you mean?" asked Tori.

"I picked up weak electrical signals," said Ron. "At first it seemed like the processing of a device, but I have been analysing the patterns and I think it might be conversations."

"Conversations?" asked Ay-ttho. "Of whom?"

"Of the Arint."

"You think some of them might still be alive?" asked Sevan.

"I think quite a few of them might still be alive," said Ron. "And very close by."

"Okay, let's suit up, Tori," said Ay-ttho.

"What about me?" asked Sevan.

"You stay here and guard Ron."

"Ron doesn't need guarding."

"It's true, I don't."

"Okay, put a suit on."

Once in their suits, Ay-ttho, Tori and Sevan took a handheld weapon each and descended the gangway to the interior of the burnt-out hulk of the wreckage of the giant ship. Ay-ttho followed the signal that Ron had pinpointed, and they discovered that, next to the broken bulkhead, was a compartment which appeared as if it was still intact.

"If you can detect the signal, Ron, why didn't the Republic ships detect it too?" asked Ay-ttho.

"The Republic were looking for the signature signals of the Mastery of the Stars," Ron explained. "They were not interested in weak signals which are practically indistinguishable from a malfunctioning computer. Besides, I was messing with the Republic scanners, remember?"

"You're the best, Ron," said Tori.

"In here," Ay-ttho signalled for the others to follow her through a slight gap in the debris behind which was an almost intact corridor and an intact door to a section of ship which appeared remarkably undamaged. "Ron? Can you scan behind this door?"

"I am detecting many weak signals. I am convinced they are life forms."

"Can the Arint breathe the atmosphere on Inic B'Campa?"

"According to my records, they can."

"Okay, let's try to open this door then. Stand back."

Sevan and Tori gave Ay-ttho some space while she shot out the door controls.

The door swung open to reveal about a hundred creatures of varying sizes, but even the largest was half the size of Sevan. They had small eyes and long snouts and stood upright on legs which seemed to end in claws. Fur covered them apart from spikes which protruded from their backs.

"Let's get them to the Mastery of the Stars," said Ay-ttho.

CHAPTER 13: DEATH ON SIRIUS

Ron sealed off a cargo bay and modified the air so it resembled the atmosphere of Inic B'Campa, then set about trying to simulate food suited to the biology of the Arint.

"We'll take them as far as Sirius," said Ay-ttho. "It's not controlled by the Republic and the atmosphere is like Inic B'Campa."

"Why is the Republic so keen on eradicating the Arint?" asked Sevan. "They seem harmless."

"It's not so much the Republic as the Cheng-Huang," said Tori. "But the Arint have been hounded wherever they have travelled in the galaxy and once trapped on Inic B'Campa, there was no way for them to run anymore."

"They put up a fight," said Ay-ttho. "And now, the Cheng-Huang is the Republic with Akpom Chuba as President."

"Will they be any safer on Sirius?" asked Sevan.

"At least they'll be far from the Republic, or at least far from the capital," said Ay-ttho.

"How long will it take us to get to Sirius?" asked Tori.

"Difficult to tell," said Ron. "There are many systems we will need to pass through, and I can't be sure from the information I gained from the Republic ships, the distance between portals."

"We're not in a rush, are we?" asked Ay-ttho.

Sevan didn't want to say anything, but he wanted to get back to The Doomed Planet and see his aunt as soon as he could.

With the Arint secure in the cargo hold and no sign of the Republic fleet, Ron reversed the Mastery of the Stars out of the wreckage of the Arint ship and took off, out of the atmosphere of Inic B'Campa and towards where the Republic charts had shown the next portal would be.

"Why is this region called strange worlds?" asked Sevan.

"Would you like us to stop at some to show you?" asked Ay-ttho.

Curious as he was, Sevan would rather get home than experience the oddities of the galaxy.

"The first portal is close, it won't take as long to get to Sirius as I had imagined," said Ron.

"I might go for a rest," said Sevan.

"I wouldn't advise it," said Ron. "If these Republic charts are to be believed, there are going to be some sights you might not want to miss."

Sevan took Ron's advice and stayed on the bridge, slumped in the chair that he was now considering his own since Tori took over the weapons chair. As he stared out the observation window, he saw they were approaching the first portal and before he realised they were passing through it.

At the other side of the portal, Sevan couldn't see anything of interest out of the window.

"I thought there would be something to see, Ron," Sevan complained. "Call me when we get there."

"Wait," said Ron. "Can you see that silver dot straight ahead?"

Sevan approached the observation window and stared outside. Ron was right, they were approaching something, but it didn't seem very impressive to him, just a silver disk.

"What is it?" he asked.

"Wait, it's Bondauzuno."

"It's what?"

"The planet Bondauzuno, watch."

Sevan watched.

"It's a bit flat for a planet, it's just a disc," he said.

"That's not the planet," Ron corrected him. "Those are it's rings."

"Then where's the planet?"

"Wait."

As Sevan waited, the Mastery of the Stars drew closer to Bondauzuno and the disc-like shape filled the observation window.

"They're huge," Sevan marvelled. "The rings."

"Yes, they are, aren't they," said Ron. "If you look closely you can see Bondauzuno in the centre. That gap in the rings, in the middle, is where Bondauzuno's moon orbits."

Sevan thought the rings were spectacular, and he was glad that Ron had made him stay to see them. He watched as they passed and then disappeared into the distance.

"Approaching the next portal," said Ron.

"What is the next system we will pass through?" asked Sevan.

"We will pass close to a planet called Chelrolia," said Ron. "The planet does not rotate and so the hemisphere which faces their star is scorching hot and the hemisphere which faces away is freezing cold. The Chelrolians live on a narrow strip of land running around the circumference between the hemispheres."

After they had left Chelrolia, they passed Aziatera which was covered in water, then came Tigromia, a planet covered in ice despite the proximity to its star.

"Why does the ice not melt?" asked Sevan.

"Because the gravity is so strong," explained Ron. "It compresses the water vapour in the atmosphere, into a solid so it never melts no matter how much it burns."

There were several more wonders before they arrived at the Sirius system. Cholvarth, which was covered in diamonds. Eonus where it rained sapphires and rubies. Paocarro which orbited its neutron star every two hours and Dichuliv where it rained glass.

"If some of these planets are covered in precious stones," said Sevan. "Why have the Republic or the Corporation not tried to colonise them?"

"They have," said Ron. "There have been many wars in the outer regions over the stranger worlds. Perhaps this is why Akpom Chuba invaded the Arint. He is maybe thinking of expanding into the outer regions. There are many other wondrous planets we haven't passed."

"There are more?"

"There is Pherimia which eats light, Strorth 08J which is bright pink, the mega planet of Zyke Z4 and many more."

"How long to Sirius?" asked Ay-ttho as she and Tori entered the bridge, having left out of boredom after Chelrolia.

"We have just entered the system," said Ron. "You can already see all three stars."

Out of the window, Sevan could see a large white star and a smaller white star.

"Where's the third star?" asked Sevan.

"Okay, I lied," admitted Ron. "It's hidden by the brightest star."

"How far to the planet?" asked Ay-ttho.

"We are almost there."

"Better get our suits on then."

As Sevan was getting dressed, he could see they were getting closer to a blue planet with an atmosphere full of clouds. As they passed through the clouds, he saw that water covered almost the entire planet with only a few small continents.

"Ron, are any of the continents uninhabited?" asked Ay-ttho.

"One of the landmasses contains a colony of Ocrex," said Ron. "There is an alternative landmass that appears to be uncolonised."

"Take us there."

Ron flew the Mastery of the Stars low over the ocean and Sevan could see large volcanoes spewing smoke into the atmosphere. As they approached the land mass, he noticed that millions of tiny stepping stones packed close together covered the coast.

"Do you know which Ocrex have a colony here, Ron?" asked Ay-ttho.

"No, Ay-ttho, it just has the signature of an Ocrex colony."

"What's wrong with the Ocrex?" asked Sevan.

"Nothing," said Ay-ttho. "I just have some unfinished business with one of them."

Ron brought the Mastery of the Stars down on a rocky outcrop, immense waves were crashing on the rocks below. All the land Sevan could see appeared barren, and in the sky was an enormous moon.

"How are the Arint going to live here?" asked Sevan. "There's nothing here."

"Don't worry, Sevan," said Ron. "It might appear like there's no food here, but there is an incredible amount of microscopic life that the Arint can sense with their electro-sensitive snouts. They are remarkably well adapted to this carbon rich atmosphere, and their hides will protect them from the high levels of UV."

"Oh, good," said Sevan, understanding little of what Ron had just explained.

In their suits, they went down to the cargo bays and led the Arint out onto the volcanic rock surface. They unloaded the food that Ron had simulated and some materials for the Arint to build shelters.

It was difficult to tell, but Sevan thought the Arint seemed grateful that they had transported them to their new home.

"We had better get a move on," said Ay-ttho. "It will be dark soon; the days are very short here."

"Ay-ttho, there is a craft approaching," said Ron, via her communicator.

"Can you identify it?"

"Ocrex."

"Here we go," Ay-ttho muttered to herself. "Get those last crates off, we need to be ready to go."

The Arint hopped to shelter under an overhanging rock as the noisy craft flew low over the Mastery of the Stars before landing on a vacant stretch of rock.

Ay-ttho, Tori, Sevan and almost a hundred Arint watched as the door opened on the strange craft and a brownish, orange creature with a vast head, large black eyes and eight long tentacles emerged. Sevan felt he had seen the creature somewhere before.

Ay-ttho wasted no time in approaching the creature, and Sevan saw that the parts of skin its suit did not cover were changing colour. The creature began waving its tentacles about and Ay-ttho responded by waving her arms around in a way that reminded Sevan where he had seen the creature before; it was on Pandoria when they were looking for the last assassins. The creature had disappeared when the Republic had attacked the planet.

After a lengthy conversation, Ay-ttho returned to the others, and the creature retreated into its ship.

"He's invited us to their colony," she said. "Let's get on board, we need to follow his ship."

"Who's he?" asked Sevan.

"Abaxax," said Ay-ttho. "You met him on Pandoria."

"Well, I didn't exactly meet him," said Sevan. "I thought he looked familiar."

They said brief and little understood goodbyes to the confused Arint before boarding the Mastery of the Stars to follow Abaxax's ship to the Ocrex colony.

"Why does he want us to go to their colony?" asked Tori.

"I think he feels bad about abandoning us on Pandoria," said Ay-ttho. "I gave him a hard time for abandoning Gwof and told him what a nightmare we had with Lopez."

"It was hardly his fault," said Tori.

"All the same."

They followed Abaxax to a settlement on the coast on the edge of a small cove where the waves broke offshore on a rocky outcrop which created a natural shelter.

Once they had landed, Ay-ttho, Tori and Sevan left the Mastery of the Stars and followed Abaxax to a structure built around a cave, close to the water. Abaxax and Ay-ttho were waving at each other all the time, and Sevan noticed that Abaxax was changing colour rapidly.

"I thought Ocrex didn't live together in colonies," said Tori.

"They don't usually," said Ay-tthoo. "But they are also fugitives from the Republic and running out of suitable environments for them."

They followed Abaxax into his cave, where he invited them all to sit. He sat down in front of them and waved his tentacles when, suddenly, his head exploded.

Tori and Ay-ttho reached for their weapons, Sevan hadn't thought to bring his, but before they could raise them, they found themselves on the dangerous end of several other weapons held by Republic guards at the cave's entrance.

"We are arresting you for the murder of President Man, his partner and her begotton, Ozli, and the President's adviser Kellen Kader and his begottons, Fenris and Zarah," said a guard.

"We didn't kill any of them," said Ay-ttho. "Let alone all of them."

"The Republic court has already found you guilty," said the guard. "We are here to implement your sentence."

"What is the sentence?" asked Tori.

"Transport by Rocket to the penal colony on Aitne."

"Not again," said Sevan.

CHAPTER 14: KIRKLAND TAKES CONTROL

The guards took their weapons and then led Ay-ttho, Tori and Sevan out of the cave and across the rocky terrain to a fleet of Republic ships which they had hidden on the far side of a volcanic rock formation.

The guards led their prisoners into a vessel where they took them to a sizable room and secured them to chairs in front of a panel of large screens.

"What's this for?" asked Ay-ttho.

"It is for the official sentencing," said one a guard. "We are setting up a link to the Republic court on Future."

"I thought the court had already made their decision?" asked Ay-ttho.

"The President wants the Republic to see that the assassins of President Man will have justice served upon them."

"President Chuba?"

"That's right. The President himself plans to be present for the sentencing."

The screens in front of them crackled into life. On one, Sevan could see President Akpom Chuba, on another were three gas filled vehicles, presumably the judges of the Republic Court, and on a third screen, Sevan recognised Kirkland.

"We are here to sentence the murderers of President Man, his partner, her begotton, their adviser and his begottons," said a judge. "We have captured them as they ran away from the scene of the crime and valiant Republic troops have apprehended them in the Sirius system."

The republic guards straightened with pride on hearing this.

"As is tradition, on these occasions," the judge continued. "We permit the guilty a brief statement to beg forgiveness from the Republic."

Everyone then seemed to look at Ay-ttho, Tori and Sevan, waiting for some form of apology.

"I'll make a statement," said Sevan.

Ay-ttho and Tori, turned to look at him with surprise.

"We intercepted a message from the first President Man saying that his co-begotton, the last President Man was planning to kill him and had deployed a troop of mechanical bowmen to carry out the assasination," said Sevan. "Ozli Man saw this message and was understandably upset, he challenged the President and his co-begetter about this. It was a very confusing period for everyone and in one particularly confusing moment, Ozli accidentally killed the President's adviser, Kellen Kader. The President twice attempted to have Ozli killed. The first was during the Republic's attack at Trinculo where Ozli was present as a guest of the Corporation, representing the President. They later sent him on a mission to the Tomorrow space station where the President had sent orders to have him executed."

"This is highly irregular for a prisoner statement," protested a judge.

"We must abide by tradition and let him finish," said Kirkland.

"Zarah Kader killed herself," Sevan continued. "President Man and Fenris Kader devised another plot to kill Ozli by tampering with his jet pack and poisoning his pish. This plot worked in that they killed Ozli Man but it also backfired because it resulted in the deaths of President Man, his partner and Fenris Kader."

"Ridiculous," said President Akpom Chuba.

"I'm afraid not," said Kirkland. "Not only does Sevan's fresh evidence shed another light on the case, but I have also received some additional evidence which I think the court will find enlightening."

"What's your point, Kirkland?" asked another judge.

"I wished to present this extra evidence to the court," said Kirkland. "I believe the court will consider it worth reviewing, as it has a bearing on the future of the Republic itself."

"If you must, Kirkland," muttered the judge.

"I would like to play you a recording," said Kirkland, giving a signal for the recording to be played.

"My crime is rotten," Sevan heard the crackly voice say. It sounded familiar. "It smells all the way to the Better Place. The murder of my own kind. There is no way to make this right, not while I am the president."

Sevan then realised it was the voice of President Man.

"My office and my union," the President's voice continued. "Can I make things right and still hold these positions? This galaxy is full of evil ways and rich criminals who avoid justice and reap the profits of their crimes by bribing their way, but they cannot do that in the Better Place. There is no deceit there, all must tell the truth about what they have done. I am trapped."

"You must stay strong, you must stick to the plan we agreed," said another voice which also seemed familiar to

Sevan. "Dispose of Ozli and I will help you to conquer the outer regions."

Sevan noticed President Akpom Chuba looked uncomfortable.

"I talk of the better place," said the President. "But my thoughts remain here on Future. Words without thoughts never go to the Better Place."

"Good," said the other voice. "Carry on with the plan as we agreed and use Fenris, he will help."

"I have another recording I would like to share with the court," said Kirkland, giving another signal.

"Have you done what we agreed and disposed of Ozli?" a voice asked. "Have you briefed Fenris yet?"

Sevan was convinced this was the voice of Chuba who looked like he wanted to leave, but guards surrounded him, Republic Guards, not his own.

"I have sent them to find Ozli and return with what remains of Kader," said the voice of President Man. "It is too dangerous to leave him on the loose, we need to put tight restraints on him. He is popular among the idiotic masses, for some reason completely unknown to me, and because of that his punishment would be noted but not his offence. Therefore, his exile must appear planned, we solve desperate problems with desperate solutions or they are not solved at all."

"Tell me when it is done," said the other voice. "I will get word to Fenris, he will be angry, you can use that anger to our benefit."

"These recordings prove that Sevan is right when he accused President Man," said Kirkland. "But they also show that President Man had a conspirator and I think you'll agree that it is clear from the recordings that the conspirator was Akpom Chuba. We traced the communications to prove this without a doubt."

Chuba made to leave, but the guards directed their weapons towards him, and he thought twice about trying to escape.

"Thank you for presenting that fresh evidence, Kirkland," said one judge. "The accused are telling the truth and that President Man, Ozli Man, Fenris Kader and Akpom Chuba are complicit in all the murders. This case is dismissed.

The screens with the three judges and the screen with the panicked looking Akpom Chuba went blank with a crackle of static. The screen with Kirkland remained switched on.

"Thank you, Kirkland," said Sevan. "Thank the Giant Cup you had those recordings."

"That's President Kirkland to you, Sevan. And there is no reason to thank me. You are still being sent to Aitne, the guards have prepared a transportation rocket for you."

"What? But we're innocent," Ay-ttho protested.

Kirkland laughed and with a flicker, the screen turned off.

The guards unfastened them from the chairs and, at gunpoint, marched them outside and past the ships to where they had constructed a rocket launcher and a rocket stood waiting.

"What the hell is that?" asked Ay-ttho.

"A penal transporter," said Tori. "They use it to transport prisoners when it doesn't matter whether or not the prisoners reach the destination."

"Oh, great," said Sevan. "Ay-ttho? Can you contact Ron?"

"I tried, but I can't get the communicator to work. Or they're blocking it somehow."

Sevan looked around, trying to estimate how practical it might be to escape, but there were too many guards to make a run for it.

The guards led them to the rocket gantry and forced them to climb the stairs until they reached the entrance hatch which they were told to enter.

Inside there was a capacity for many more prisoners, but they strapped themselves to the nearest chairs.

"Have you got a plan?" Sevan asked.

"Not a very good one," said Ay-ttho. "If you have a suggestion, now would be an excellent time to share it."

"I don't have a plan," said Sevan.

"Me neither," said Tori.

"Then we'll have to go with mine," said Ay-ttho.

"Does your plan involve being fired into space in a rocket?" asked Sevan.

"Yes, unfortunately, it does."

The guards left and sealed the hatch. Sevan could hear them descending the staircase.

"How did Ron not spot a rocket launcher on his scanners?" asked Sevan.

"Maybe they were screening the signature of the site," Tori suggested.

"So, your plan really does involve us going into space?" said Sevan.

"Yes," said Ay-ttho.

"And how are we supposed to escape once we're in space?"

"These rockets are just designed for aim and shoot," said Ay-ttho. "They'll just point us at Aitne and fire, they're not bothered about whether we get there."

"How is that supposed to reassure me?"

"We just have to wait until they fire us into space, then they'll forget about us. Then all we have to do is find a way of turning the rocket around."

"What about the Mastery of the Stars?"

"They'll leave that for the Ocrex."

"Oh, great, the ship might not be there when we get back."

"Ron will look after her."

The rocket shuddered and Sevan realised they were firing up the gravity displacement device. There was a metallic clunk as the gantry released the rocket and then they were pressed into their seats by the rapid acceleration as the rocket launched.

There were no windows in the rocket, but they knew when they were outside of the atmosphere because of the weightlessness.

"Will this rocket survive re-entry?" asked Sevan.

"You've always loved asking questions, haven't you," Ay-ttho complained. "Yes, it will survive re-entry, it's made from tough stuff. We just need to find where the gravity manipulation unit is."

As soon as they released themselves from their straps they floated around the compartment, looking for access to other compartments on the rocket.

"It's completely sealed," said Tori.

"Not completely," said Ay-ttho, removing her helmet. "There is a breathable atmosphere so there must be a way of recycling the air."

"Like vents?" asked Sevan.

"Under the seats," said Tori.

Ay-ttho helped Tori rip up a seat which proved quite a challenge in microgravity. They used the body of the rocket to push against and forced the seat from its mounting, which ripped up a section of the floor. With the section removed, they could see that beneath the floor was a compartment which contained air ducting and cabling.

Ay-ttho and Tori looked at each other and then at Sevan. Tori removed his helmet.

"Sevan's the smallest," he said.

Sevan took off his helmet.

"What do you mean, I'm the smallest?" he asked.

"Sevan? Do you know how to reprogramme a gravity manipulator?" Ay-ttho asked.

"I don't even know what a gravity manipulator looks like, let alone how to reprogramme one."

"I'll have to go," said Ay-ttho.

"Can you get in there?" asked Tori.

"There's only one way to find out."

Ay-ttho began stripping off her suit while Sevan and Tori tried to rip up more of the floor.

"Even if you can turn the rocket around, how are we going to land it," asked Sevan.

"Don't worry about that," said Tori. "All Ay-ttho needs to do is programme a new location and the rocket will go there and land itself."

"What could go wrong?" said Sevan, to himself as much as Tori.

Ay-ttho pulled herself into the hole in the floor and along the cavity towards the end of the compartment.

"I can see it," she shouted back.

"Can you reach it?" asked Tori.

"Just about. This should be simple if I can just..."

Sevan fell to the floor as he suddenly felt his normal weight return.

"What happened?" he asked Tori, who seemed to expect this.

"Ay-ttho has asked the gravity manipulator to manipulate the gravity inside the rocket, now she just needs to change the manipulation on the outside."

"Of course," Sevan sighed.

"Okay," Ay-ttho shouted back along the cavity. "I've just added the location, the rocket should change trajectory in three, two..."

Sevan was thrown to the floor again as the rocket lurched wildly.

"What happened?" Tori shouted to Ay-ttho as the rocket lurched again.

"I don't know. Maybe there is an anti-tamper device. It seems to be completely out of control."

CHAPTER 15: THE RUNAWAY ROCKET

"What do you mean, it's out of control?" asked Sevan, trying to hold on to a seat as the rocket lurched from side to side. "Does that mean we are just floating in space until we die?"

"You are such an optimist, Sevan," said Tori.

"I'm not surprised," said Sevan, losing his grip and falling over again. "Here we are floating in space with no food or water. How do they expect their prisoners to get to Aitne?"

"I don't think they expect them to get there. I think most of those they transport die on the journey."

"Great!" Sevan let out an enormous sigh, as he pulled himself into the seat. "Even if, by some blessing of the Giant Cup, Ay-ttho can get that thing to work and get us back to the Mastery of the Stars, we are now fugitives. We won't be able to return to the Republic, we'll be wanted all over the region."

"I wouldn't worry about that. They'll assume we died on the way to Aitne. I doubt anyone will come looking for us."

"I hope you're right."

"Can you do anything about it?" Tori shouted into the cavity.

"I'm trying to bypass the anti-tamper mechanism," Ay-ttho shouted back. "But if I get it wrong, I could lock us out of the system permanently."

"Where did she learn to do all this stuff?" asked Sevan.

"It's a lengthy story," said Tori.

"Hold on tight," Ay-ttho shouted. "I'm about to activate the bypass."

Sevan held on tight to his seat and a moment later he was glad he had as the rocket turned over completely and he hung from the seat which was coming away from the floor which had become the roof.

The rocket lurched again and righted itself, dumping Sevan on the floor again once more.

Ay-ttho crawled out of the cavity.

"That should have done it," she said as she climbed back into her suit. "The rocket should take us back to the Ocrex colony on Sirius."

"What about the Republic troops?" asked Sevan.

"I doubt they're still there," said Tori. "I'd be more worried about what the Ocrex might have done to the Mastery of the Stars."

"Ron can take care of them," said Ay-ttho.

"I hope so," said Sevan. "He wasn't that successful against the looters on Daphnis."

"They were professionals," said Ay-ttho. "The Ocrex are amateurs, at stripping a ship, that is."

Sevan tried to make himself comfortable as he waited for the rocket to complete the journey back to Sirius.

He hadn't been comfortable for very long when an alarm briefly sounded from somewhere.

"We'd better put our helmets on and strap ourselves in," said Ay-ttho. "We're approaching the atmosphere, the descent could be rough."

Sevan made sure he strapped himself in very well. Ay-ttho had not lied. The rocket shook vigorously as it made its descent to the planet's surface. He felt unbearably hot as the compartment heated. His suit was not designed to compensate for situations like these, the Mastery of the Stars had bigger suits which would have been better, but they hadn't imagined they would have been in this situation when they had left the ship.

There was a violent jolt and a terrible scraping noise as the rocket skimmed across the surface of the rocky terrain. Then came a loud crack as the rear section of the rocket was torn off, Sevan could see debris being thrown up into the air behind him as the rocket was being torn to pieces.

It veered to one side and rolled, pieces being thrown off with every revolution. Sevan soon lost sense of which way was up until what remained of the rocket came to a rest against the face of a volcanic mountain side, at which point he knew with certainty that the wreckage had come to a rest upside down.

"At least we need not open the hatch," said Ay-ttho, releasing her straps and landing on her feet on what remained of the roof of the rocket.

"That was fun," said Tori, performing a similar acrobatic exit from his seat onto his feet next to Ay-ttho.

Seven released his straps, got his leg caught, and tumbled out of the seat into a pile at their feet.

"Nicely done," said Ay-ttho. "Let's find the Mastery of the Stars."

They emerged from the wreckage on to a barren stretch of volcanic rock, littered with debris from the landing.

"It should be just around here," she said, skirting the rock face while the others followed.

Sure enough, as they circled the mountain, they passed the ruins of the rocket gantry, then the Mastery of the Stars came into view. There was no sign of the Republic ships but signs of fighting and smoke was rising from the direction of the colony.

"Be careful," said Ay-ttho. "Something has happened. I'll try to contact Ron before we approach the ship. Ron? Can you hear me? Ron?"

"I can hear you, Ay-ttho," Ron's voice crackled over her suit's communication device.

"We are near the ship, Ron. Can you open the door and let us in?"

"I can, but be careful, the Ocrex are around and they have been trying to damage the ship, I have been fending them off with the cannons."

"Okay, let's go," Ay-ttho, led Tori and Sevan across the rocky terrain.

They were halfway between the safety of the rock face and the entrance to the Mastery of the Stars, when they saw the Ocrex emerging from the smouldering remains of the colony. The three of them had to duck as they ran to avoid the cannon fire that Ron was aiming above their heads to scare away the Ocrex.

As they ran, Sevan could see the door of the Mastery of the Stars opening and the gangway lowering. It had barely reached the rock floor when they reached it and leapt aboard. Ron closed the entrance immediately, continuing to fire the cannons at the Ocrexwho were trying to make a dash for the open door.

Ay-ttho, Tori and Sevan made their way straight to the bridge and stripped out of their suits.

"Let's get out of here," said Ay-ttho.

"I'm afraid that's not possible," said Ron. "The Ocrex did some damage to the ship, we have to repair it before we can leave."

"Great," said Sevan. "Anything else we should know about?"

"Would you like the good news or the bad news?" said Ron.

"Give us the good news."

"The good news is that you are not fugitives. I picked up some Republic transmissions. They know you are no longer heading to Aitne but President Kirkland has announced that you have already served your sentence."

"And the bad news?"

"The bad news is that they now classify you as ex-convicts which may prohibit entry into certain systems."

"I can live with that," said Ay-ttho.

"There is more bad news," said Ron. "There is now a power struggle between President Kirkland and the supporters of Akpom Chuba. The Republic is on the brink of civil war and they have stationed patrols on all portals entering the Republic."

"Why should we worry about that?"

"With the portals guarded, it might be difficult to sneak back into the Republic to return to The Doomed Planet as we had intended."

"I see your point," Ay-ttho sighed. "I need some food and some rest, does anyone object if I retire to my quarters for a while? One of us will need to keep watch in case the Ocrex return."

"Can't Ron keep watch, still?" asked Sevan.

"He has done an outstanding job looking after the Mastery of the Stars but he could not prevent the Ocrex from damaging the ship by himself, he needs someone to help him."

"I will take the first watch," said Tori. "You two get cleaned up, and eat, and rest, I`ll be fine."

"Thanks, Tori," said Sevan, as he followed Ay-ttho off the bridge.

*

Tori sat in the weapons chair, staring out the observation window. He was fiddling with a small piece of metal, it was the lump of shrapnel they had dug out of him after the accident at Trinculo. He placed it on the control panel and sighed.

It had been a long night, and it was time for Ay-ttho to relieve him. He thought Ay-ttho's obsession with security was unnecessary. Ron had looked after the Mastery of the Stars while they had been trying to turn around the rocket, so why the paranoia?

The Ocrex had spooked Ay-ttho. That could be the only explanation. There was nothing to fear from them, the cannons on the Mastery of the Stars could easily keep them at bay.

"Who's there?" said Ay-ttho, entering the bridge.

"Identify yourself," said Tori, seeing a purple figure approaching.

"Identify yourself."

"Ay-ttho?"

"The same."

"You are very prompt," Tori checked the instruments on the control panel. "It's exactly time for your watch."

"Get some rest, Tori," Ay-ttho slumped into the pilot's chair, her antennae flopping over the side of her face

"Great, I'm fed up of this stupid watch business," Tori grimaced with all three sets of his teeth.

"Nothing happened then?"

"Nothing."

"Get some rest then. If you see Sevan, tell him to hurry up."

"I can hear him now."

Sevan sauntered onto the bridge.

"Morning Ron," said Sevan, still half asleep.

"Good morning Sevan," said Ron, the ship's navigational computer.

"You're not going to say good morning to us then?" asked Tori.

"Good morning Tori and Ay-ttho," said Ron.

"Not you, Ron. Sevan."

Sevan squinted at Tori.

"Is it just me who feels like this has happened before," he asked.

"Oh, I'm off to bed." Tori stomped off the bridge.

"Sleep well," said Ron cheerily.

Sevan slumped in the weapons chair that Tori had only recently vacated and stared out of the observation window at the towering buildings which seemed to cover every available space on Future, the planet which served as capital for the Republic.

"Don't let Tori see you there," Ay-ttho warned.

"He doesn't frighten me," Sevan retorted.

Tori stomped back onto the bridge and Sevan leapt out of the chair. Tori marched towards him but stopped short, retrieving a small object from the control panel which he pocketed before turning about face and stomping off again. He stopped at the entrance to the bridge and turned.

"Yes, this feels familiar," he said.

Sevan breathed a sigh before going to sit in another chair.

"What's up with him?" asked Sevan, gesturing in the direction Tori had just left.

"I think he's upset because he took the first watch."

"I don't blame him. I'm not entirely sure why you are so worried, Ay-ttho."

"I don't trust the ocrex," Ay-ttho looked like she was fed up of explaining herself. "I don't want to spend any longer on this planet than we absolutely have to. Once we have finished the repairs, we can leave."

Sevan liked the sound of this. He was very keen to get back to his home, The Doomed Planet, and visit his aunt. Now that the jump point would have a Republic patrol guarding it, it might be more difficult to get through and so he was keen to get started as soon as possible.

*

Enjoy this book? You can make a big difference.

Reviews are the most powerful tools in my arsenal when it comes to getting attention for my books. Much as I'd like to, I don't have the financial muscle of a large publisher. I can't take out full-page ads in the newspaper or put posters on the subway.

(Not yet anyway)

But I have something much more powerful and effective than that, and it's something those publishers would kill to get their hands on.

A committed and loyal bunch of readers.

Honest reviews of my books help bring them to the attention of other readers.

If you've enjoyed this book, I would be very grateful if you could spend just five minutes leaving a review (it can be as short as you like).

Thank you very much.

Get a **free** exclusive bonus chapter to **Shipwreck on Lysithea**, only available here.

Building a relationship with my readers is the very best thing about writing. I occasionally send newsletters with details on new releases, special offers and other bits of news relating to my novels.

If you sign up to the mailing list, I'll send you an exclusive bonus chapter to Shipwreck on Lysithea.

You can get the epilogue, for free, by signing up at: https://BookHip.com/JKLGGT[1]

---

1.   https://BookHip.com/JKLGGT%20

Still not ready to leave Sevan?

Swordsmen of Angetenar
Book Five in the Mastery of the Stars series
To be released 25th April 2021
Pre-order now[1]

---

1. https://buy.bookfunnel.com/8e1zrtaub7

ABOUT THE AUTHOR

M J Dees is the author of five novels ranging from psychological thrillers, to dystopia, to historical to humorous fiction, as well as the Mastery of the Stars sci-fi novella series. He makes his online home at www.mjdees.com[1].You can connect with M J on Twitter at @mjdeeswriter[2], on Facebook at www.facebook.com/mjdeeswriter[3] and send him an email at mj@mjdees.com if the mood strikes you.

---

1. http://www.mjdees.com

2. http://www.twitter.com/mjdeeswriter

3. http://www.facebook.com/mjdeeswriter

ALSO BY M J DEES
Living with Saci

When your partner goes missing and you become the prime suspect, what do you do?

Living with Saci is set in the sprawling metropolis of São Paulo, Brazil. It tells the story of Teresa da Silva, an overweight, depressed, drink dependent, and her struggles in the city. Estranged from her daughter, who lives with the ex-husband in England, life seems to constantly deal Teresa a bad hand. She begins to wonder whether the mischievous character from Brazilian folklore, Saci, might have something to do with it. Events seem to be taking a turn for the positive when she meets Felipe, who asks her to marry him. But when he disappears, Teresa finds that she is the object of suspicion.

<u>Get it now</u>[1]

---

1.   https://buy.bookfunnel.com/7moc52jtuk

Living with the Headless Mule

A car crash and an encounter with a priest turns Teresa's reunion with her daughter into a life-changing struggle.

Teresa is a drink dependent, middle-aged Brazilian who just wants to be reunited with her daughter but her ex-husband's accidental death leads to a fight for custody of their child.

Bob is a pastor with secrets. He makes Teresa an offer which seems too good to refuse until the truth about him is revealed. Teresa must choose between her daughter, the pastor, or her life.

Book two in the Teresa Da Silva series, this spicy psychological suspense novel, Living with the Headless Mule can be read before or after M J Dees' debut novel, Living with Saci, for which this is a prequel/sequel.

<u>Get it now</u>[1]

The Astonishing Anniversaries of James and David: Part One

How do you know if you have achieved success? No matter how successful he becomes James doesn't feel happy. Meanwhile, his twin brother, David, seems content regardless of the dreadful, life threatening events which afflict him year after year. The Astonishing Anniversaries of James and David is as much a nostalgic romp through the 70s, 80s and 90s England as it is a shocking and occasionally tragic comedy.

Get it now[1]

---

1.   https://buy.bookfunnel.com/upraz4oono

When The Well Runs Dry

In a country divided by civil war, one city stands above the chaos. Since the system collapsed, citizens are struggling to survive. Marauders are destroying what little is left. However, not everyone is ready to surrender. The Alder and her loyal supporters find themselves caught in a life or death struggle to save, not only themselves but also those around them. The future of the nation is at stake. When The Well Runs Dry is the first book in M J Dees' dystopian series set in a future where resources have all but run out. Read this book while there is still a future in which to read it.

<u>Get it now</u>[1]

Fred & Leah

At a time of war, soldiers are not always the only casualties.

On September 3rd, 1939, Fred knew he would have no choice but to go to France and fight. However, when he found himself among the thousands of men stranded after the Dunkirk evacuation, he had no idea when he would see his wife Leah and his two children again.

Leah is left trying to raise her two children by herself but, even she can't stop the bombs from falling on her street.

M J Dees' fourth novel and his first historical novel, Fred and Leah, is based on a real-life love story of two people whose lives were irrevocably altered by war.

<u>Get it now</u>[1]

---

1.   https://buy.bookfunnel.com/jvqhvcibuu

DEDICATION

To the Bard, whose stories are timeless and spaceless.

ACKNOWLEDGEMENTS

I am indebted to the following for their help. My beta reading team and my advance review team, especially Chris Wells, Daryl Schumann and Carol Moon for spotting last minute changes.

COPYRIGHT